MODERN GOTHIC

LERAH MAE BARCENILLA
MICHAEL BIRD
PETE HARTLEY
EDWARD KARSHNER
ROSE BIGGIN
LAUREN ARCHER

First published 11th October 2024 by Fly on the Wall Press
Published in the UK by
Fly on the Wall Press
56 High Lea Rd
New Mills
Derbyshire
SK22 3DP

www.flyonthewallpress.co.uk
ISBN: 9781915789167
EBook: 9781915789242

The right of Lerah Mae Barcenilla, Michael Bird, Pete Hartley, Edward Karshner, Rose Biggin and Lauren Archer to be identified as the authors of this work has been asserted in accordance with the Copyright, Designs and Patents Act 1988.
Typesetting and cover design by Isabelle Kenyon, imagery Shutterstock.

A CIP Catalogue record for this book is available from the British Library.

CONTENTS

A GLASS HOUSE FOR ESTHER
MICHAEL BIRD

Every year, before the anniversary of the tragedy that devastated the Hampshire estate of Rackonton, I requested an interview with its reclusive owner, Mr Herbert Cardew. An heir to a cotton milling fortune, he held a disinclination towards exposure, so the public perceived that his silence regarding this disaster was a tacit admission of guilt. In my letter, I cited my experience as a reporter at *The Middlesex Oracle*, and argued that if his version of the story were to remain undocumented, many would believe he had evaded incarceration due to his high status. I added that, if he wished to choose myself as an agent for such a confession, I would be a less vicious questioner than a haughty prosecutor or a village gossip.

It was a compliment to my persistence that, in the fifth year of my entreaty, my editor presented me with a positive reply from Mr Cardew. The handwriting was jagged, and problematic to decipher, which implied he was either sick in body or mind, but not significantly deranged for this to be an inconvenience to our conversation. Without adding further details, he summoned me to his winter residence in Camberwell Grove, a leafy annex of London once known for its exclusivity.

A shaggy oak and flowering shrubs framed the tall iron gates, which fell open at my touch. Facing me was a boxy townhouse from the reign of the third King George, where each upper level hosted windows smaller than the one below, creating the illusion of magnitude.

After ringing the bell, I was ushered inside by a broad woman with a nervous temperament, dressed in the fashion of a servant from two decades past. As she took my hat, coat and cane, I mentioned how pleased I was to make her acquaintance. In response, her narrow eyes scrutinised me with suspicion, perhaps aware that my bonhomie was not entirely sincere.

No paintings or etchings hung on the walls, and the varnish of the floors was spoiled with dents and scratches. This indifference to luxury was not an uncommon feature of our nation's richest men, some of whom understood how the retention of wealth depends on not spending on frivolity.

But this was not the reputation of Mr Herbert Cardew. Prior to the catastrophe, he was known as one of the Empire's most profligate figures – a celebrated sponsor of charity, and a consummate entertainer of princes and lords. The maidservant presented a morning room bathed in such gloom that my eyes required time to adjust. Windows should have offered a view onto the rear garden, but were replaced by a brick wall, plastered over and painted white. An oil lamp lay on a small round table, illuminating no more than the outline of two armchairs, one of which was occupied.

"Please join me," came a rasping voice.

"Thank you, sir," I took the seat opposite.

"I trust there is enough light for you to take record of this congress."

"I hope it will be sufficient."

"There will be tea shortly."

"That is very kind."

"I expect you are wondering why I reside in such bare lodgings."

"It caused me some surprise."

"I assure you that I do not lack income."

"That was not my assumption."

"Yet there is much of my former life that I have relinquished."

"It can be liberating to give up such vanities."

"Vanities? What *vanities*? I speak of ambitions."

"I did not wish to offend," I said, "and beg your indulgence as I seek to comprehend the events of which I am ignorant."

Cardew inhaled a long breath, his throat rattled, and a wheeze slipped from the pit of his lungs. But this was no impediment to his speech:

I inherited properties that stretched from the suburbs of London to the English Channel, and my family had multiplied this wealth with ventures in Canada, Africa and the Raj. Thus, I was in possession of a bank balance which was so extraordinary that my single vocation was to ensure it was exhausted.

A part of this included spoiling my only child, Esther, who was soon to be of womanly age. For many years, I had been estranged from her mother, who chose to stay in Paris, a city I found disagreeable to my moral and physical constitution. At that time, Esther was attending a radical boarding school that nurtured and developed her aspirations, so for the short periods she spent in my company, I had to ensure she was subject to rigorous stimulation.

She loved nature, and would prefer to play with the hunting dogs or ponies than with her friends or cousins. This interest extended to a fascination for the zoological gardens of caged animals that had become fashionable in our great cities. Yet she confessed that she felt these creatures to be miserable in a climate as unbecoming as that of England. So, I intended to build a refuge that better accommodated the sensitivities of such beasts.

In my instructions to the architect, I demanded a square mile of glass and iron, rising six levels and converging in a hemisphere, matching the dimensions of Il Duomo in Florence. Our home was to be no more than a trim of brick that skirted three sides of this conservatory, leaving the southern approach exposed.

To heat such an expanse, I enlisted the best engineers from my old family firm. Below ground, railways with minecarts transported coke to boilers, which fed hot water into perforated pipes. Through grills in the basement, this network poured steam inside an enclosure that spread over six hundred acres. No feat of technological progress had ever been attempted on such a scale as Rackonton. Once the structure and mechanics were complete, the hot-house welcomed its first guest.

"Father," said Esther, her pupils widening to absorb the amplitude, "this place leaves a great impression on me."

"I am glad to win your approval."

"I rather think of it as a symphony of metal and light."

"That is very poetic."

"Yes," she said. "I am blessed with a poetic disposition."

"Then we must find more to inspire you."

The botanists were first to arrive. From West Africa, East India and the Amazon, they brought coconut, date and rubber trees. At the centre of the greenhouse, they carved out a large pool, floating with giant water lilies, strong enough to hold a child. Ferns, cacti, coffee and banana prospered alongside leaves shaped in lobster claws, and the open palms of the fly-trap. From inside the folds and roots of these plants, tiny monsters hatched. Termites rampaged through timber, and the air swarmed with huge flies, the size of a baby's fist. Their expansion encouraged spiders to stir from their hideouts – some hairy as a bearded paw and others flat, with tendrils that slithered along the earth.

Because our conservatory had no walls, all the rooms of our residence were exposed to its spectacle. A screen of glass occupied one side of the kitchen, drawing room, dining room, library and stableyard. As my staff washed linen, dusted bookshelves, brushed the horses and polished the silver, they could not escape the backdrop of creepers and threads twisting against the windows, terrorised by scores of insects. The sounds of rustling and cutting, chopping and buzzing, warbling and chafing were a constant accompaniment to us, day and night, along with a bizarre, alien fragrance that danced between the sweet and the putrefying.

Esther sat in her bed chamber, reclining on a chaise-longue, admiring the scenery, and I was happy to find her so thoroughly engaged.

"It is extraordinary," she said, "to see plants that grow on plants, that, in turn, grow on further plants."

"Each has its own character."

"For me, there is much beauty in the vines."

"And these," I pointed to the hanging stem of a liana. "They skirt every trunk, dine on the trees, and when they are finished, strangle them."

"How very horrible," said Esther, her gaze lingering on the verdant cords.

Once I saw the garden was flourishing, the nature of my orders from abroad began to change. At the entrance to the mansion came boxes of sloths, turtles and frogs, snakes in wire cages, and wooden crates with butterflies nesting in fruit. After our new additions had settled, I sought out larger mammals and reptiles.

In the marble hall was a glass panorama, one hundred yards in length, and straddling the full height of the habitation. Two iron doors lay at its centre, necessitating a pair of manservants to unhinge its locks, before the portal opened slowly, in the manner of a medieval fortification. At their side, painted steps led to a giant chute, through which the stablehands dispatched animals into the forest.

Chimpanzees climbed to the canopy, and broke off sticks to dig out vermin from the timber, while caiman, capybara and anaconda explored the dirt until they reached the lake.

Esther was enamoured by the lemurs, who stretched out their thin arms, and glided from branch to branch. Their speech enchanted her, as they bleated, purred, croaked or wailed in a high, human-like pitch. She ran through the house, racing from ballroom to library to living room and back again, and shadowing the lemurs in the trees. It was uncertain whether she was following them, or they were in pursuit of her.

One afternoon she rushed into my study, and spoke fervently of her observations of these primates.

"They were gathered around an object of interest, at first invisible to me. Each of them picked up a stone and pounded the target of their attention with disciplined savagery. The crowd dispersed, and on the floor lay a long, black and bludgeoned corpse, which I understood to be a boa constrictor. Its mouth was open, and its tongue and fangs frozen in a cry for help."

"Was this disturbing to you?"

"My sympathy for the reptile was equal to my satisfaction at seeing the lemurs vanquish their predator."

One early Autumn morning, in front of the mansion, a carriage had abandoned a single crate on the steps. Inside flapped an angry bird, knocking its beak against the slats. Esther picked up the box, and saw that it contained a toucan. She was so amused by its orange bill, yellow breast and blue feet, that she named the bird Harlequin.

"This is too beautiful for the forest and shall take up residence in my chamber," she told me. I was reticent at first, but she insisted, and soon Harlequin was installed on a perch in her quarters, where it snapped its jaws for attention. I instructed our servants to feed the toucan a mix of fruit and insects, but

Esther quickly assumed this duty. When I knocked on her door to say good night, I found her spearing cockroaches on sharp pieces of wood, and holding them above the bird's beak.

However, Esther herself was attacked by Harlequin, who left small scars on her arms and face. In addition, the toucan expelled liquid waste, black and pinkish-red, in whatever location it so desired. I told Esther we should let the animal into the wild, but she argued that she would dedicate hours to its house-training, and, if this proved ineffective, she would find herself another bedroom.

The summer was over, and Esther returned as a boarder to her school. A trusted maidservant adopted the role of feeding the toucan. As she entered the room, the bird leapt on her, and lurched at her plate. It had a special fondness for raspberries, and loved to fling the pulp across the Chesterfield couch and the drapes of Esther's four-poster bed.

One morning the servant found the bird on the ground below the window to the conservatory. Its beak had cracked and its wings were broken. Blood was splattered on the glass. It was shivering, deeply in pain, but too damaged to plead for help.

In tears, the maid detailed to me what had happened, and said she was willing to suffer the consequences of her failure to attend to the bird. I assured her she was not to blame, and asked her to empty the creature into the chute. Its fate was now the business of the forest.

I wrote to Esther, informing her of Harlequin's misfortune. It was my belief that the bird had spent days watching the hot-house alone, and had sought its own method of entry, but in vain. I tried to break this news with sympathy, as I was concerned it might cause her turmoil.

But I was heartened when she wrote back the following:

Dearest Father,

You must not fret about the sad demise of Harlequin. I will always remember his glorious beak, the vibrant colours of his plumage, and the tortured but caring eyes of this loving bird. Forever in my thoughts will be the times we spent together, with his claws gripping my shoulder, or smoothing his bill across my cheek, as though I were a fellow member of his species.

I have no doubt that he had frustrations with me, indicated by his habits of expelling faeces on my nightgown, or hurling pieces of mango in my face. Yet whenever I closed the drapes to my bed, and his cawing in the early hours tempered to a sleepy moan, I felt the deep sense of companionship that you hoped I would find with the animal kingdom.

Perhaps this is not the manner in which I — or indeed Harlequin — would have preferred him to meet his end. Yet I must come to terms with such unpleasantness, because as it is certain that all toucans must die, so it is also certain that life will offer me other toucans,

Yours sincerely,

Miss Esther Cardew

I was so impressed by her mature response, that I rewarded her with a marvellous present for Christmas.

Passage was bought from the Congo Basin for a family of pygmies. Entering our hall, the parents were shivering in raincoats, borrowed from my driver, while their son and daughter wore ragged dresses from our serving maids. As they walked through our marbled hall, they seemed terrified by the expanse of the building, and puzzled by the furnishings. Once they viewed the sheer enormity of our garden, theirs to occupy as they deemed fit, they uttered cries of euphoria, and removed their western clothing. The children fled to the trees, climbing on the branches as though this was an opportunity for limitless play, while their parents scouted the terrain in bare feet, and dirty linen around their waists. Within a few days, at the edge of the lake, they built a hut from thick shoots and mud.

Esther was fascinated by the new addition to the conservatory, and spent the week before New Year with a telescope in her room, following the progress of the family. The days wore on into late winter, and she returned to school, coming back to Rackonton only for weekends. But in early March she entered my study, seeking counsel on a matter of grave concern.

"I have observed the jungle people for some time," she said. "They do not move from their home, nor do they hunt in the pool or among the trees. When they venture outside, it is clear from their wasted bodies and slovenly demeanour that they are hungry."

"I, too, have noticed a degeneration."

"Father, do they not like the creatures and fruits the forest offers?"

"I fear they did not consume such a diet in the Congo."

"Then we have been mistaken."

"This does seem to be the case."

"Perhaps," said Esther, "it would not be unkind of us to provide them with some food?"

When the pygmies were passing near the kitchen, my head cook waved to them to come to the hall. Through the chute, she dispatched bread and cooked mutton, and pointed to her open mouth. Esther and I watched the family crouch on the floor, and greedily devour the meal. Mother, father and the two children attempted to chew, but spat out the roast meat, and returned to the camouflage of the trees.

*

It was summer. My daughter was in her eighteenth year. We had presented her to the Queen at court, and planned to follow this with a grand ball at our estate. I invited masters of industry, arts and science, as well as lords and parliamentarians. Each arrived with their wives and relations, including a not insignificant supply of unattached men.

The women were dressed in flared skirts, embroidered blouses and wide-brimmed hats, and the men in black suits, bow ties and tight cummerbunds. However, the heat of the conservatory caused them to perspire, and their skin to chafe against the collar and waist. Our staff served a menu of oysters au gratin, lobster bisque, duck breast, foie gras, beef terrine and Champagne, which helped dull the stultifying humidity.

Esther descended our staircase in a floor-length gown of rippling silk, her neck glowing with a chain of pearls, and her brunette locks falling about her shoulders. I was blushing with intense pride, as it is impossible for a father to recognise anything less than unimpeachable beauty in his only daughter, as she reaches womanhood.

When the meat dish was served, a stablehand brought in a large cow on a rope. For the guests, the presence of the source of their meal was an irony which prompted a simmer of amusement.

The cow was led beyond the tables to the far end of the room. Two manservants wrenched open the locks to the portal. Slowly, the gates parted. The stablehand, nervous, stepped cautiously into the balmy enclosure. Leaving the rope hanging around the cow's neck, he scurried to the hall, and the manservants shut the gates.

No pasture lay here, only a carpet of decaying leaves, ravaged by termites. The cow retained a static poise, except for the swing of her tail through a swarm of flies. Her hide was baking, her lungs heaved, and her mouth hung agape. Aware that something was about to occur, the guests put down their cutlery, turned away from their plates, and regarded the animal.

The first to arrive was my most recent acquisition, and the perfect present for a debutante — a young male jaguar. Leaping from a high branch, the big cat pounced on the back of the cow. A gasp fell from the guests, followed by a short applause.

Still the cow did not move. Nor did she bellow in fear or pain. The jaguar gripped the bovine's head in his paws, and dug his fangs into the skull.

The legs of the beast buckled, and she tipped over, while the feline jumped free and landed on the forest floor. Cleaving into the cow's belly, the jaguar pulled out links of intestines, and feasted on the offal, smearing his face in red. Once the carnivore lost interest, the chimpanzees arrived, then the lemurs, and finally the insects. The scent of fresh death spread through the dome, as each resident sought to gorge on remains of the kill.

I was seated next to Esther, as she watched the proceedings, occasionally placing her gloved hand on my leg in approval.

"I hope you will return to see your new gift," I said.

"Naturally."

"I can spoil him with a goat, a pig or even a wild boar, which may pose more of a challenge."

"I shall look forward to such moments."

"But with your new status, there will not be many opportunities like these."

"Oh father," she said, "I will always make time for my jaguar."

When we served the dessert, only the carcass of the cow was left, with blood glistening on her bones. At this stage, all the guests had turned away from the conservatory. Quite a few had left the dining area, and were lying on couches in our drawing room, while I had dispatched the servants to find smelling salts and other remedies for anxiety.

Following her coming out, Esther was resident in Camberwell Grove for the duration of the Season, while I remained at Rackonton. At this point, my wife returned from her long sojourns on the continent to assist her only daughter in finding a fiancé. Once a week, Esther wrote to me, elaborating on her progress. Although I was overjoyed to receive such letters, I was filled with trepidation before reading their contents.

She talked of how tiresome and superficial were men, and how their intentions towards her concerned her physique and financial means, but never approached her private passions. I was pleased with this realisation, and responded by informing her how we had imported four female jaguars from Brazil. Within a week, the male had three separate wives at each corner of the conservatory, all of whom were pregnant and no longer wanted to continue their acquaintance with the father. Finally, he made his way to the last, but she rejected him. This did not stop his perseverance. Every night, we could hear him, whining at the bottom of her tree, while she lounged on a large branch near the canopy, licking her paws.

Esther wrote back to say 'the poor boy has nowhere else to go'.

Soon my daughter was introduced to a promising suitor at a garden party in Hertfordshire. Clarence Montague was from a family which possessed ample quantities of land near Lincoln. He was of dignified stock, even if he was only a second son, and in line for a less than significant inheritance. As my grandfather was a self-made industrialist, and my father an investor in farming, it was customary for our *arriviste* class to match our offspring to anyone with an ancient title, as this would secure our place among the nobility.

Through Esther's correspondence, I detected she was quite taken with the young man, who had come down from Oxford two years previously, towered over six feet, and was athletic in posture. His current occupation was at the Inns of Court, and it was thought he would become a barrister – a profession for which I held some admiration. Montague enjoyed hunting, spending time in the countryside and expressed an interest in venturing into the Amazon, so Esther believed it was possible their interests could find sympathy in one another.

The engagement was much talked about in society. Yet after three months, Esther wrote a letter which pained me greatly to read.

Dearest Father,

I am addressing this letter in confidence. It is not for further distribution, and to ensure such secrecy, once you have read and interpreted its contents, I entreat you to reduce these pages to ash.

As I have previously informed you, I am currently engaged to a Mr Clarence Montague, a well-established gentleman, who has met with your approval regarding our future nuptial arrangements. Although I knew Mr Montague to be a man of experience in relations with the opposite sex, it appears he has been spending several nights a week in Somerset, with the young widow of a certain Lord Harris, who recently died in a grouse-shooting accident.

The rumour was delivered by my own mother, an individual with whom I understand you communicate little.

This deceit caused me much distress, which I demonstrated to mother in a not entirely calm manner. In reply, she stated that I would be unable to restrict such a becoming and wealthy man as Montague to myself.

As you have taught me, I must be direct and honest in my exchanges with all persons, regardless of their position in society. Therefore, I confronted Mr Montague with the accusations. His first response was to deny any relationship with Lady Harris, but I pushed him on the issue, and he expressed apologies for his initial negation, stating that he did indeed call upon the widow. However, he insisted it was a matter of friendship, as she had sought consolation in him after the untimely passing of her husband. Sceptical of Mr Montague's abilities as a specialist in the grieving process, I sanctioned him from further contact with this woman.

I believed my reaction had been steadfast and fair, and was pleased that the matter no longer seemed to be of concern to our acquaintances and relations.

But a week later a friend informed me she had seen the two of them at a ball in the city of Bath, where they were conversing with great intensity.

Because I realise that my ultimatum has failed, I understand an alternative approach is necessary. The ideal course of action is to bring him to Rackonton, to ensure that he is welcomed into our family, and made more aware of its unique character.

I hope you will be well-disposed to assist me in this endeavour to provide a swift solution regarding the current obstacles to my marital success,

Yours sincerely,

Miss Esther Cardew

On an October evening, two of my carriages arrived at the door of our mansion. One was carrying my daughter, and the second Mr Montague. Once I welcomed Esther, he descended from the taxi, dressed in tweed hunting attire, and offered me an exuberant and informal greeting. As we entered the house together, the young man congratulated me on my "far from modest lodgings", adding that he had "rarely seen such architectural eccentricities". Esther ushered him into the hall to show him the vista. Most impressed by our ambitions, he could not believe he was watching primates clawing over the canopy of a palm, and eating freshly-picked bananas.

"How dissimilar this is to a zoological garden," he stated.

"Indeed," I replied. "The creatures are at liberty to eat and play as they desire, with little interference."

Esther took the arm of her fiancé.

"I would be delighted to accompany you on a stroll through the hot-house," she said.

"That would be an excellent idea," said Montague.

"Allow me to change from my day clothes into something more loose-fitting to accommodate the humidity."

"Please take your time."

"Such a delay should not stop your own investigation."

"I shall explore with pleasure."

Two manservants opened the iron locks. The gates creaked, and closed behind the aristocrat with a sudden thud.

Watching from the window, Esther removed her gloves, and placed one hand on the glass for a few seconds. Montague waved back and turned to the deep forest. With his hunting cap pressed down, and his boots pulled up, he braved the overgrown track, swinging his cane to push away the thicket.

A few days later I welcomed a constable into my home, who wished to converse on the subject of a freak disappearance. Together, we retired into my study, for sherry and a cigar. I outlined how Montague had received a letter on the evening of his arrival, from a sender unknown to me. This summoned him to Bath, and he left early the next morning to catch the train. I did not offer the policeman the opportunity to search my mansion, because such an invitation may have prompted a certain suspicion.

For Esther, the loss of a suitor with a prominent place in society was not easy to explain to a community blighted with gossip. Her mother was afraid that her name would be tainted, so it was decided that the two of them should take a long trip abroad — starting with the Grand Tour of Europe, and then adventures further afield. I was happy to finance this journey, providing I would not have to engage in any correspondence with my errant spouse.

The carnivores were the first to die. The body of a jaguar was crumpled against the glass of the pantry, its face and eyes ambushed by flies. A few hours later, only a ribcage and skull remained. The chimpanzees thumped the windows of the conservatory with strips of wood and thigh-bones, trying to smash their way out. Into the chute, my manservants dispatched fresh meat from our abattoir, and it was devoured with enthusiasm, but did not stop the trend of decline. During this time, the pygmies vanished, and I believed they had become victims of the hungry primates. Without a predator, the capybaras and anteaters bred faster, but they failed to survive.

The palms wilted, their fronds fell, and the lush emerald and amber turned to a sick yellow and dirty brown. Rot set in, and fungi grew across the earth and dead plants, bringing a stench of sulphur and methane that permeated through the glass. Yet the ants multiplied. They carved up every falling leaf into fragments, which they carried in long lines to the seat of their queen.

I looked out at my new dominion. How could I offer this vile exhibition to my illustrious acquaintances? A territory where big cats and monstrous reptiles once roamed had become no more than a scrapyard for insects.

One night in late March, I was awoken in my chamber by a violent blast. The windows rattled. The walls shook. Voices were calling from the patio. Dressing with haste, I ran downstairs, where a manservant informed me that a furnace had exploded. Smoke was billowing from the grills of the hot-house, and fire was sprawling through the tunnels. The coal shovellers were asleep in their cottages, miles from Rackonton, and too far to remedy the situation quickly. In the kitchen, I assembled my staff, and ordered them to administer to the emergency — but no servant would dare enter the underground vaults to put out the burning boiler. Every one of them explained that the filth that had gathered there was unspeakable to behold. No threat I could issue was severe enough to make them reconsider their decision.

So I took an oil-lamp, spread a damp cloth across my face, and fought the tide of smoke swelling in the tunnels. My brow was dripping, and my head was dizzy from the pollution, yet I persisted. Below, to the sides and on the ceilings, creatures had settled in the darkness. I brandished my torch above, and encountered a throbbing mass of gleaming fur, pink skin, tiny sharp teeth and wet eyes. Bats dangling from the ceiling screeched at the light, their tongues seething.

Along the walls shone moist pupa, traces of silvery-green secretions and black excrement. Powdery webs smeared my forehead, and warm prickles of hair grazed my scalp, neck and shins. Trapped in gossamer were the carcasses of rats, wrapped in silk, their eye-sockets gouged, and bellies ripped open. Inside their wounds lay clusters of eggs.

As the flames advanced, my head was bathed in perspiration, and my lungs clogged with smoke. Coughing hard, I struggled towards the source of the mechanical failure. Reaching a boiler room, I encountered mangled iron and piles of glowing coal, burning fiercely. I planned to push a minecart of coke along the railway, at a distance from the fire, to prevent further detonation.

As I wrenched back the cart, I heard a hiss from the tracks. With reluctance, I passed my torch in the direction of the shrill utterance. A tangle of baby vipers flailed upon a carpet of white grubs. Within this chaos shivered a human foot, smeared in black. I shifted the lamp closer. Naked and hiding from the glare was Esther.

She did not respond to my protestations to move, and seemed dazed by a lack of breath, so I placed the wet rag from my face upon hers.

As Cardew leaned forward, I observed his features for the first time. The gentleman carried a stern, but not unsympathetic appearance, and his hands and neck were mottled in reddish pink.

"I expect she had absconded from her tour in Italy or France, and had anonymously sought passage homeward," he said. "I believe her mother did not have the fortitude to inform me about her failure as a chaperon."

Resuming his reclining position, Cardew turned his head to the bricked-up windows, tilted his gaze low, and continued:

Lying upon a bed of arachnids and cocoons, and feeding off such vermin, had transformed Esther's body into a pale version of itself — blue veins pulsated along her arms and legs, and her skin was strewn with bruises and bitemarks. But her eyes were bright and resolute, as I held her close and stumbled through the blaze.

"I wanted…" she spoke weakly.

"Shhh."

"I wanted to be…"

"Not now."

"Away from everything."

Breaking through dense smoke, we left the chambers and climbed the steps to the mansion's driveway. An intense flame rose from the heart of the building, caressing the sides of the dome, and punching the glass.

Shards splintered into the air, and rained upon us. Cradling Esther tight, I limped as far as I could from the building. Fire pumpers had arrived from town, but their vehicles stood idle, while the drivers stared, dumbfounded, at the torrid sky. I slumped on the lawn of our estate, and looked at Esther. The blaze illuminated her face.

"We can build this again."

"Oh father, more glorious?"

"Ten levels higher, two miles wider."

"Because there is so much to discover."

"Every tree, plant and animal."

"In our home."

"Only for us."

The edges of her mouth formed the contours of a smile, yet as her eyes narrowed, I could not be certain if this was due to a blissful thought or sudden pain. Her arms slipped from my grasp, and I dragged them closer to me. Lying on the grass, I clung to every part of her that still beat with warmth.

*

The nib of my pencil was stubby and the writing thickly-drawn. The tea had arrived, and stayed untouched. When Cardew's face had been animated, it almost reached the light of the oil-lamp, but now it fell into the shadows of the armchair. I thanked him for his time and sincerity, adding that I expected this account to be printed, albeit in an edited form, in the April edition of the *Oracle*.

The next morning, I was intent on verifying the truth of this story using my own investigation. Thus, I found myself in the first-class carriage of a steam train to Hampshire. Alighting at a village halt, I was pleased to find a horse-drawn carriage at my disposal. In the front seat hunched a grey-whiskered driver in a heavy black coat, its tails stained with mud. I offered him a generous sum for passage to the site of the mansion, and he accepted with stoic accord.

"I understand the manor was a rather grand affair," I said to the coachman, as the chassis struggled with the uneven roads.

"It's not what it was."

"Are there still labourers on the estate?"

"Few be willing."

"I hear the farmland is of great quality."

"There be other fields to plough."

It was a pleasant day with few clouds in the sky, and I felt fortunate that my profession allowed me the opportunity to indulge in such trips in the bracing air of the countryside. Above the road was rolling pastureland and the outline of a man-made structure. At first its appearance was not dissimilar to that of Roman remains. As we approached, the stonework increased in size, and assumed the dimensions of a medieval castle.

"I'll take you as far as that there gate," said the coachman. "The 'orses will go no further."

Dismounting, I informed him that I would return within the hour. Soon I found the trace of a gravel path, overrun with thistles, that led uphill to the site. Here I hoped to meet tenants who could corroborate Cardew's recollections.

A stretch of rubble extended either side of me. At its mid-point, where the front entrance must have risen, were twisted girders and cracked pillars of white stone. On deeper inspection, I identified contours of brick around an expanse of rocky ground, but there was no dome to challenge the masterpiece of Florence.

It was empty of humankind, with one exception. On a stack of fallen masonry stood a boy in a sleeveless jacket of ruddy fleece, and with burned skin, probably due to a childhood spent outside. A few yards away, sheep were scattered on knolls of grass and stone.

"Young lad," I called out, "are you a former hireling of Mr Cardew?"

Refusing to acknowledge my presence, he walked to the southern exit, making a clicking sound with his mouth. A border collie circled the sheep, prodding their rears with its snout.

I persisted in following the boy. As I moved closer, I saw his face was wrinkled to such a degree that I realised, despite his height, he must have been older than myself.

"If you have a few minutes to talk," I said loudly, "I would be prepared to offer some recompense."

Around the exit, a web of metal ascended a hundred yards into the air, forming an arc, where broken panes still hung. With his back to me, the shepherd wandered out of the ruins and onto a plain. Here was a shack and sheepfold, built from the debris of the mansion. Outside stood three short figures, surrounding a steaming pot on a campfire.

The sheep rambled across the mounds of rusty beams, fractured tiles and charred bricks. One strayed on a grill, bleating at the distance, uncertain whether its hooves were trapped. The collie ran over to assist, nudging the sheep out from the wreckage, under the arch of iron and into the open country, where the animals followed their master to his home.

LIVID
PETE HARTLEY

Have you ever had one of those dreams in which you know you are dreaming yet, despite all your efforts, you cannot wake up? You have become your own dungeon. You are a prisoner of your sleeping self. You might never awake.

The first time I heard those words, I knew they had been said to me before. I did not hear them on the previous occasion because they were spoken in a dream. Sounds in a dream are silent.

The second time those words were spoken, I was watching a performance. It was seven months after the first time they had been directed at me. A light came up on the stage, and there she was: the woman from the dream.

I knew it wasn't actually her. Nothing in the theatre is actually what it seems, not even the truth. She wasn't as real as her first manifestation had been; the one my mind had been made to exhume.

The cone of light that defined her was narrow and ethereal. It was as if her existence was being illuminated by someone who knew what a mere impression of her would mean to me. The chair from which she stared had furled spines that were longer than hers, forcing her into a forthright posture. Her limbs, however, told of resignation.

"Only you can release you, and you are not responding," she said, without lifting a finger.

As each sentence announced its entrance, my mind reintroduced its former appearance before me. That face, those fingers, that blouse, that brooch, that voice. The speaker was

27

the same person, saying the same words, but not in the same place. The last time I saw her she was not on a stage and I was not seated in an auditorium with seven hundred others.

Her outfit was more conventional than fashionable. She wore a cream cotton blouse with a two-inch collar, fastened at the back and studded with a deep blue brooch at the throat. Her earth-brown skirt was worsted and durable. She would have slotted unobtrusively into the high street multitudes at the start of the second decade of the twentieth century. This occurred during the month of November in 1913; an ominous year.

She shifted in her seat, aligning herself even more directly towards me. Then the sharpened words came.

"You will not feel my grip on your scapula."

Those words sliced into me. I had heard them before but they had not been part of the dream.

"You will never see the lacerations."

A rational curiosity elbowed its way to the front of my shock. What would the others in the audience make of that remark ? They would be storing the comment, presuming it would have some implication later, while I knew it was being said to reawaken a confidential recollection of something from my past. I began to perspire. Her voice reverberated. Deep within the ellipsoid of my cranium, the beat of my pulse became audible.

"My kiss will be a firebrand," she said.

Upon hearing that my lips burned, scorched by their own salt.

"You will not feel my teeth on your clavicle."

The sweat from my neck raced for my spine.

"You will not feel your collarbone snap," she said, and that was enough to render me unconscious.

I had frequented the music hall in Sawdoctor Street on multiple occasions, and I had been in the manager's office several times, but never in a semiconscious state.

They administered smelling salts, which spurred my responsiveness whilst simultaneously reinstating the shock that had removed it. I am convinced that the scent of sal volatile had been a component of the dream from which I had been told I would not awake.

The cornice of the office had been domestically neglected. Spiders' strands had become dust bunting. I was semi-prone on a chaise longue, brushed velvet in texture, sage in hue, and worn in condition. Miss Westhead gave me sweet tea, under Mr Crayford's supervision. My collar had been removed and placed, with its bone and brass studs, alongside the contracts on Mr Crayford's desk.

I remember making bungling apologies and hearing Mr Crayford's and Miss Westhead's fervent dismissal of them. The sugar in the tea had been counterbalanced by brandy. Gradually, that concoction roused me sufficiently to partially recall what had caused my collapse. Once I became aware of where I was and to whom I was indebted, I was anxious to speak to the person that had brought about my predicament.

I complimented Mr Crayford on the potency of his bookings. He smiled indulgently, and I asked if I might meet with the lady performer to offer my appreciation of her skills. It was Miss Westhead's turn to indulge me, laughing warmly and encouraging me to drink more of the restorative brew. I was not going to be dissuaded, however. Even in my unsettled state, I was conscious that I must seize the opportunity to discover why the woman on the stage had repeated precisely the words I had previously dreamed, and then wed them to others that I had heard spoken in very private circumstances. I pressed my request again.

Mr Crayford remained polite but his charming tone took on a steely firmness. No such act had appeared that night, he told me. Miss Westhead added her adamance. At the moment when I had fainted, she said, everyone else in the auditorium was watching a magician.

"An illusionist," said Mr Crayford.

I took the last tram to the eastern suburbs of the town. It terminated a mile short of my destination which was the horseshoe arc of Whitebeam Avenue, whereon stood three detached properties that were too old to be desirable and too viable to be demolished. Interspersed between the residences were towering tree sentinels. Some were examples of the eponymous whitebeam species, but the majority were horse chestnut. All had shed their leaves and hence their limbs slashed starkly against the tombstone stratus. The hour was far from civil, but here lived the only person who could help me.

The delay before my knock was answered suggested that even the maid had retired for the night. Nightcapped and shawled, she set the door ajar.

"Yes?"

"My name is..."

"I know who you are, sir."

I too, knew her. "I apologise for the lateness, but I wondered if I might see Mrs Moritz."

"Is it urgent?"

"No."

"Well then..."

"But it is a matter of some desperation."

She toyed with the door.

"Deep desperation."

"I'll ask," she said. "You'd better step inside."

She requested that I wait in the hall and went upstairs. The night was not especially cold for November, and I was now indoors, but my tummy trembled and my shoulders spasmed. Perhaps there had been too much brandy in the tea, but it was

more likely that I was still in a state of shock. I felt another
belt of sweat about my brow, and went to remove my hat, only
to discover that I had left it at the theatre. A hint of ammonia
returned to my sinuses, and I steadied myself against the jamb
of the sitting room door.

"Go through to the parlour, if you would."

I had not heard the maid come down the staircase, nor had I
seen her do so, despite the fact I thought I had been looking that
way all the time.

"There is a fire in there. Mrs Moritz will join you shortly.
May I bring you some warm milk?"

"Thank you. Warm milk would be most agreeable."

"Would you like a little sugar in it?"

"Erm…"

"And a little brandy?"

"Brandy?"

"You look a little pale, sir."

"Pale?"

"It's Demerara."

"What is?"

"The sugar. Bring the colour back to your cheeks, sir."

I have no recollection of leaving the hallway and entering
the parlour. The next I can remember was my shoulder being
shaken and someone speaking words that I did not recognise but
nevertheless knew what they meant. I opened my eyes. I was
immersed in an armchair. It felt too deep. My shoulders were
hunched so that my scarf holstered my neck, setting my dignity
ajar.

"I've warmed the milk, sir", said the voice, as sound and
meaning were reunited. The maid placed the glass on the
occasional table. A fluted lamp stood upon it. Its lemon light was
thin but stronger than the crimson afterglow from the fireplace.

"Thank you." I shuffled my posture in the direction of decorum.

"You might want to remove your scarf, sir."

"Yes," I said and tugged it free.

"Oh!" she said, staring at the place where my collar should have been.

"Ah," said I, fumbling with embarrassment. "It is in my pocket. They removed it at the theatre." I rose awkwardly and began rooting rigorously.

"Not on my account," said another sound, that sound, and there she stood. The lamplight was inadequate for me to see the detail, but I knew the gown must be exotic blue. It was wrapped snugly and comprehensively over whatever she wore for sleep. Her hair was loosely tied back with a paler blue ribbon. The ebony tresses had more strands of pewter than I remembered, but it was, of course, the noble cheekbones, the hazel eyes and the almond lips that deeply delighted and disturbed me. I expected another assault of nausea but none came.

"Mrs Moritz, I must offer my..."

"Of course you must not," she said grimacing benevolently. She proffered her hand. I pressed it to my lips for a fraction longer than might be thought proper. "Now take off your coat, sit down, and drink some of your milk. Una, you might bring me a tumbler of the same."

"With brandy, ma'am?"

"Generously."

"Yes, ma'am."

Una left us. The shared solitude was too charged. I found that I was rather pathetically clutching my collar. I passed it from one hand to the other and produced the studs from my coat pocket, then looked towards her as might a child to a mother. We were, in fact, of a similar vintage.

"Alban," she said, speaking as a mother might, "I have spent thirty years in the theatre. I am not in the least disturbed by the sight of a man's throat."

My collar bone tweaked.

"How can I help?"

I reached for her hand again, but she side-stepped to stand behind me and lift my coat from my shoulders.

"Sit down, drink the milk, and tell me of your despair."

I sat in the chair and she on the sofa, and I told her all that had transpired, starting with the dream from which I thought I might never awake, culminating with the information being relayed on stage, by a person who added secret intimacies known only to me and to one other: the woman with whom I was now speaking. Furthermore, the visage of the woman in the dream, and the face of the woman on the stage, were imperfect replicas of each other, and of the one on which my eyes were currently fixed.

Lazuli was not in the least perturbed by my account. She was, by nature astute and wise, and by profession courageous and intrepid. Lapis Lazuli had been a double act whose stage illusions were Persian-themed. Lapis was the magician, and the one who garnered the glory. Lazuli was his glamorous aide. She was the decoration, the distraction and the promotional attraction. She was also the secret of his success, the cause of his demise, and the sole inheritor of his estate. We had collaborated before.

I cannot remember Una re-entering the room with a glass for her mistress, but by the time I described my collapse, Lazuli had drained her drink. She listened to my story attentively, but also with an air of indulgence, implying that she already knew it, or had guessed at it.

"Dear Lazuli," I implored, "can you possibly explain how such a deception could be delivered to a sole spectator among a crowd?"

She pursed her lips in consideration and slowly inclined her head. "It would appear incongruous," she said.

"Did I dream it then?"

"Perhaps you did," she said.

"But it was so vivid. And continuous. A dream is not continuous, its flow is interrupted. Not so with this. Prior to my fainting, I can recall everything in detail as a continuous whole. I felt the downstage draught that follows the raised curtain. I saw the silhouette of the stagehand as he positioned the seat, heard the entrance of the invisible performer, heard the creak of the chair and the snap of the spotlight — and there you were. Or rather, there was something that was almost you. I was shaken by the fold of your mouth as you formed your sentences, and the tender rasp of your breath as you projected the word firebrand."

Her eyes held memory; her attitude compassion. She placed her hand on mine. "I have no desire to haunt you," she whispered.

I placed my hand on hers. "I would not mind in the least, if you did."

Her smile was short-lived. "But..."

"But what?"

Her eyes inclined diagonally towards the drawn velvet drapes. "Someone else might."

After that it was oscillating reminiscences and reassurances. She remained of the view that my haunting had been manufactured in my mind, but pledged that she would make inquiries to establish what had happened in the theatre. She knew backstage people. Nothing would take place on the boards without their knowing.

The carriage clock on the mantle pealed midnight. Lazuli insisted I stayed until morning. I was too enchanted, and too uneasy, to object more than convention demanded.

The room to which I was assigned, I presumed, had once been used by Lapis Moritz, Persia's magnificent enchanter, as the playbills had proclaimed him. He was a magician and a mesmerizer, who wore an ochre turban and a purple kaftan edged with a gold braid and embellished with oriental swirls. Lazuli, his living gem, was almost always in shades of blue from turquoise to violet, but mostly in that rich lazurite hue of her name. Almost always. Sometimes she would appear in startling white for seven seconds or less, then back to blue in an instant. Yes — that swiftly. I've seen it. I timed it. I reported it. That's how I grew to know that she was the real magician of the show. What she could do was not superhuman; it was far beyond that.

A candle does not cast light, it merely keeps the unseen at arm's length. My flame illuminated the bedroom in shuffling instalments. The décor had a scenic fakery one would associate with a stage show, a quality heightened by the sweeping gloom of my light. The drapes were terracotta in colour, but showed as midnight sand in the dimness. The rug presented as Persian. The furniture purported to be mahogany and ebony, but I suspect its appearance was a result of stain rather than from natural grain. The tallboy put me in mind of the revolving cabinet that Lapis had used in his act. Lazuli had switched from a sapphire to a white dress in less than three revolutions of that, and back again in just one. Incredible.

The dressing table matched the wardrobe in shade, its triple mirror splaying the feeble beam from my candle and multiplying the shadows behind me. A fire had been set in the grate, but, I surmised, had lain unlit for several weeks. Perhaps for several months. Since Lapis died.

Despite the lack of heat, the room did not feel especially cold. There was a kind of dry caul in the air.

A cream flannel and towel had been placed over the foot of the bedstead. The off-white bed sheet, beneath a purple counterpane, had been turned back, inviting but also forbidding, like a shroud on standby. A jug and basin, the former with a hairline crack alongside the spout, had been placed on a grand chest of drawers. That furnished my mind with another illusion in which Lapis utilised a horizontal cabinet. Lazuli would switch from shelf to shelf, one above, one below, in less time than it would take to fasten up then unclip and pivot down their hinged front panels: four seconds at most. For the final reveal both shelves would be exposed, with no Lazuli in sight – until she emerged from the adjacent wardrobe bedecked in a jewelled shift that had earlier been seen alongside her, folded on the bottom shelf.

I washed my face and neck. Of course, I had no nightwear and so opted to sleep in my undergarments. If sleep was to be permitted. I had no desire to extinguish the candle, and did not do so until I had transferred the flame to the nightlight in a smoky crimson vase on the table by the bed. I doubted the wax would last until dawn.

To my surprise, I awoke, and hence deduced I must have slept a little. How long, I knew not, but the nightlight had shrunk less than could be discerned. The sheen in the room was not crimson now, however, but sifted saffron. I had heard no knock, no clink of handle, no groan of timber or squeal of hinge. Yet there she was, beside my bed, bearing the fluted lamp, wrapped in the same dressing gown, but seeming slightly shorter in stature. Perhaps she was barefoot? I didn't look.

She appeared a little younger but much more steeped in experience.

"Are you comfortable?" she asked.

"Quite comfortable," I assured her.

"In mind?"

"Not entirely," I admitted.

"Ah."

This Lazuli was not inclined to reassure. I considered her distracted, and wondered if she was, in fact, sleepwalking. I knew the apocryphal dangers of waking a sleepwalker, and while I doubted their veracity, I did not dare to risk testing the theory.

"Most kind of you to accommodate me," I said, struggling to think of anything more pertinent.

"Most kind of you to accommodate me," she responded. The ambiguity of that remark was architectural. It confined me in expectation but confused me with its directness. It hinted at past mysteries wrapped in promises of devotion.

"I do not speak of that," I said.

"You'd be wise not to," she said.

"I do not speak of it," I said, "to anyone."

"You will never see the lacerations," she whispered, and all my recouperation was undone. I began to sweat again, and flush alternately hot and cold. My shoulders twitched.

She stepped closer and leaned over me.

"My kiss will be a firebrand," she said.

My lips dehydrated. Hers sported the texture of overripe grapes. She bruised them on my forehead and, as she did so, the neckline of her gown bowed forwards and I saw the unnatural kink in her collarbone.

When I awoke again, the nightlight had gutted. I could not even see the ceiling. I stared at it determinedly, willing it to pull into focus, but it would not. The darkness in the room was without flaw, unnaturally so. I wondered if I had awoken within sleep. I reached for the nightlight and my grip instantly and accurately found its aperture. I probed its inners with my middle finger and found a cast of cold wax. I considered fumbling around the fireplace for matches or hauling apart the drapes to admit moonlight. I did neither. I lay there remembering what had happened that night and questioning how much had actually occurred. Before long, my mind settled on seven months earlier, when I had submitted my notice of the performance of Lapis Lazuli. The one that led to the end of the magic show, the death of the magician, and the liberation of his accomplice.

It was the launch of the Easter season, and such was the reputation of Lapis that he had been awarded a three-week residency, topping the bill. He was enjoying a highly lucrative contract. My paper had dispatched me to review the opening night. I had seen him thrice before, and with each viewing I became more and more convinced that the real skill lay not with the master, but with his second. He should, perhaps, be credited with the invention of the illusions and with the showmanship that secured their successful delivery, but it was the astonishing ability of Lazuli that was both the engine and the fuel of the magical machinations. Without her athleticism, her flexibility, her dexterity, her speed, her scrupulousness, her deflection, her attraction and her lightening comprehension, there would be no illusion, no incredulity, no visceral surprise and no success. I said as much in my review, and that, I later understood, was the public spark that touched a flame to private powder.

Those remembrances did nothing to settle me back towards sleep. I could not see any part of the room in which, I presumed, Lapis had slept and in which I could no longer find sleep. The unseen walls secured me. The unseen door might no longer exist. Beyond the window, which might no longer be there, something tapped intermittently, but also incessantly.

Lapis stood before me beyond the end of the bed. My mind contested that I could see him, as there was no light by which he might be illuminated. Then I deduced that he did not require illumination. His presence was luminous.

He did not speak. If he had done so, I would not have recognised his voice, for I had not heard him speak while he was alive. He never spoke on stage. The whole act was conducted to eastern melodies played on western instruments by the orchestra. Only Lazuli spoke, and only after the penultimate trick, to introduce the final illusion and to proclaim the genius of her partner, who was, by implication and by her nomination 'the Great'.

Now Lapis the late stood at my feet, not speaking but staring, knowing my role in his tragedy, accusing, condemning and committing me. Then he was not before me but about me. I was in bed within him. Yes — within him. He became a bone sarcophagus and I his undead cadaver. As a mummy in its casket, I was encased within the petrified form of the magician. His rock kaftan enclosed my body, his fake Persian slippers, now fashioned from stone, secured my feet. His ceramic skull encased my cranium. I could breathe but could not move. I could think but could not act. I must rest, but not in peace.

I felt I was falling, plummeting into a canyon, searing towards a collision in which my bones would shatter and then remain permanently splinted within their ossuary. I feared I would be preserved in pain.

My cocoon became hot. I smelled smoke. I thought I might choke, or be broiled alive. My arms refused to respond. I summoned a surfeit of will and butted the inside of my jailer's skull repeatedly. The stone bone broke and my eyes saw dusky air. The window drapes were haloed with soft grey splays and amber banners flicked across the ceiling. I heard cracks and tasted slack odours of smouldering coal. The fire had been lit. My arms moved, almost of their own volition. I peeled back the counterpane, blankets and sheet and stepped onto the purportedly Persian rug.

I tugged apart a two-foot split in the window drapes. The day was still dark, but incompletely so. Winter dawn was underway. I recovered my waistcoat from the chair on which I had laid my clothes and clicked open the pocket watch chained to it. It was twelve minutes past eight.

The room was much colder than it had been the previous night, but the fire had caught well, the flames were growing and the kindling faggots were starting to collapse. I guessed that Una must have been in. It was a thoughtful service, but also, perhaps, a polite nudge to not stay in bed too long. The glow was so comforting that I spent a few moments crouched close to the grate, savouring its gifts.

I washed my face at the basin, reattached the collar to my shirt, and dressed. I could not find my tie, and deduced it must still reside, along with my hat, in the theatre manager's office. I rehearsed my apology for my slovenly appearance, but after descending to the dining room, I discovered my host was not in residence.

"She's gone to the theatre, sir," said Una.

"The theatre?"

"On your behalf. May I serve you some porridge?"

"My behalf?"

"To recover your hat and establish what occurred there last night."

"Ah, yes."

"Some breakfast, sir?"

"How kind, but I am already late for my work."

"Mrs Moritz said she would call at the newspaper office first, sir, and explain that you are indisposed."

"Indisposed?"

"But most likely will report later today."

"Most likely."

"She asks that you remain here until she returns. Porridge, sir?"

"Thank you. That would be most agreeable. And thank you for lighting the fire."

Una appeared perturbed. "Which fire sir?"

"The fire in my room."

"In your room?"

"Yes. Most considerate of you. Thank you."

"For lighting it sir?"

"Yes."

"Not I, sir."

"Then who?"

"There is no one else, sir. What time was it lit?"

"Half an hour ago — if that. What time did Mrs Moritz leave?"

"Before seven, sir."

"In that case," said I, "it could not have been her."

The porridge was invigorating. Una also served tea and toasted crumpets. I asked her to join me at the table. She was reluctant to do so but I insisted and she sat opposite me, though the table seemed suddenly much longer. I told her that I remembered meeting her on my previous visit to that house.

"How long have you been in service here?" I inquired.

"Here, sir? Since Mr Moritz purchased the property, some, well, it must be nine years ago."

"And where were you before that?" I asked.

"I travelled, sir."

"Travelled?"

"With the family, sir."

"Family? Which family?"

"The Moritz family."

Moritz, had been Lapis's surname, or at least the one he went by. Lazuli had told me, that while she was from Persia, he originated in Pershore, a market town in Worcestershire. Lazuli, had long purported to be Lapis's wife, though they had never legally married. To tour their act and lodge together without such a pretence would have been unacceptable to many landlords. In reality, their wedding had never been celebrated or consummated nor, I understood, by either part desired. Una's role puzzled me.

"You travelled with the act?"

"I did, sir. Round the music halls."

Lazuli had informed me of their history prior to their tour of provincial theatres. "And with the circus?"

"Sanger's Circus, sir?"

"That's the one." A theory clicked into my mind. "Were you a performer? A contortionist?"

Una stretched a grin and giggled. "I can see your supposition, sir, but no. I was never in the circus. Fetching and carrying, and carting – that were me. That were my family."

My theory had been dispatched before it was even unwrapped. When it comes to apparently impossible stage illusions, the obvious explanation lies in the use of a double. Whiles Una's stature and complexion did not bode well for that role, I had begun to wonder if the arts of personal decoration had played their part in exceptionally clever ways. She had firmly scotched that solution. Then she rejuvenated it.

"I did help with the deception, though."

My appetite for food was suddenly suspended. "You did? Pray tell."

"I should not, sir."

"It can do no harm now, Una. The act is no more."

"Even so..."

"It would be an of exceptional service to me."

"It's not what you might think."

The table between us now appeared shorter.

"Please explain."

"It was after they'd had left Sanger's and started the music halls. You know how popular they became. Folks speculated, like you, on how on earth Lapis could accomplish his tricks. There had to be a double, they said, or maybe even...a twin."

"A twin?"

"Folk were fighting to get into the stage wings to see how it was done. So Mr Moritz redesigned the apparatus. There were screens and drapes. It took longer to get things ready. I helped. Started cookin' as well. They took me on permanent."

"Screens and drapes."

"Behind, sir."

"Yes — upstage."

"That's right."

"I remember. So it was more than decoration. It was to hide the mechanics from backstage."

"No, sir. It were cleverer than that."

"How so?"

"There were nothing to hide. I know. I were there. There were nothing to see. Lazuli — Mrs Moritz — squeezed into some tight spaces but she never moved between boxes. The screens simply fooled folk into thinking that she did. But she never — well not for the, you know, the truly spectacular stunts."

"I saw her."

"No, sir."

"Then there must have been a double."

"Not in the music halls, sir. Not in the theatres."

"But I saw it with my own eyes. That breath-taking conclusion when Lapis separated the cabinets by ten feet or more, and Lazuli lay down in one and came out of the other."

"No, sir."

"And then she went back in that cabinet and appeared immediately behind me at the rear of the auditorium."

"She was still in the first cabinet, sir."

"Then there must have been a double!"

"No, sir."

Then Lazuli's voice stung us both. "Thank you, Una."

"Yes ma'am."

Una did not look at her mistress, who neither of us had seen come through the door. She stood, bobbed a demi-curtsy, and went to the kitchen. I was so transfixed that I had forgotten to stand. Lazuli wore the blouse with the brooch on the collar, and the heavy skirt that she had worn when I had seen her likeness in the theatre the previous evening. Why was she not at the theatre now, or at the newspaper office? She could not have been there and back so swiftly.

"So now you know," she said.

I didn't and told her so. "I thought you had gone into town," I said.

"I'm not there," she said.

"No."

"Nor am I here."

"What?"

"Neither here, nor there."

Her stance was a tad lopsided, with one shoulder a little lower than the other. I remembered my manners, and pushed back my chair.

"Don't get up on my account," she said. "If you do, you might fall down again."

I stood. "What on earth...?"

"Not there either," she said, and without moving at all, was suddenly much closer, which she couldn't be, because the table filled that space. I expected, nay I craved, that I might lose consciousness again, but I discovered that, no matter how hard one might try, one cannot faint at will. She reached for me and placed her fingers on my eyelids. She closed them as if I were a corpse. It made no difference. I could still see her. Then she pressed harder and the pain pushed my eyes back into my most bitter-sweet memory, of my first meeting with Lazuli, and the part I played in her greatest deception.

Once again, I had the abysmal sensation that I was falling, falling, falling, followed by the staccato imposition of distorted recollections, reordered, replayed and reconstituted into immediate frustrations and terrors. Hotel rooms occupied by the uninvited, threats reiterated, deadlines issued. Lazuli was kind, considerate, desperate, inconsiderate. Lapis was unspeaking, uncooperative; unalive.

Rather than confuse you with that labyrinthine dream, let me cogently relate the proceedings of nine months earlier and hence describe the conception of a life sentence which, I fear, may perpetuate beyond my grave.

De Luca's coffee house was well-known to the theatre trades, but not to me, for it was some seventy miles away on the east coast. My editor had approved the trip because of the local connection to the story.

Lapis Moritz had been found at the foot of a cliff. His head was broken. This discovery had been made less than seven days after his spectacular three-week run at the Sawdoctor Street Music Hall. Moritz had gone to the coast to negotiate a summer season. News of his death had come through on the wires, shortly after I had received a personal telegraph from 'The Genius Gem' asking for a meeting at De Luca's. The signature was a phrase that I had used to describe Lazuli in my review. Three trains were needed, but I was able to keep the rendezvous set for five in the afternoon.

"I knew you would come," Lazuli said, after the proprietor had redirected us to a small room on the first floor. There were only three tables in that room, and Giuseppe assured us that we would not be disturbed. The coffee was, without doubt, the strongest I had ever consumed. Lazuli was in full mourning: black coat, black dress, black hat. Her white blouse was pinned at the collar with a brooch, which should, according to accepted decorum be white or cream, or black, but was, of course, Persian blue. There had been much weeping, I could tell, but behind the weariness of lamentation, a great joy flourished in her soul.

"I owe you so much," she said.

I was confused, and wanted to know all I could about the demise of her supposed husband.

"We rowed continuously," she pressed, "from the moment he read your review. He detected, that the audiences aimed their loudest applause at me. I objected, and said that I had changed nothing in my performance, and that they clearly still thought him to be the maestro, but he would not have it. He was now in my shadow, he said. I had stolen the bright heart of the limelight. I insisted that was not true."

"Well, I think you might have done," I said. "As was your due."

"Not true," she maintained.

"Very true," I countered. "But pray, tell me about the cliff."

"He was pushed," she said, without the slightest hesitation. She pinioned my pupils. "By his wife."

I glanced towards the door, and scanned our room terrified that she had been overheard. "In a moment of temper?"

She considered my question, and then replied with a response that I think she had previously established. "The impulsive is a much-misunderstood action. It is not an instigation, but rather a conclusion."

"You'd had enough?"

"Some might say so."

"No one can prevail forever," I said.

"Youth is a portrait against which we all fade," she said, her Persian rhythms adding spice to the phrase and preserving the proverbiality of it. "Everything became more difficult. Sooner or later the difference would have become apparent."

"Not now," I said.

"No," she said, and her face bloomed with expectation.

"But..." I stuttered, "you've just...imparted something..."

Her face switched to a more expectant expression. "That's why I need you."

"What?"

"I trust you, Alban. May I call you, Alban?"

"Of course."

"You will transcribe the story, perfectly truthfully, from witness accounts, all honestly imparted, of how three days ago, while my husband took the coastal path I was here, in this very room. I had a two-hour conversation with a former circus comrade, before she and a gentleman acquaintance of hers kindly escorted me back to the hotel, to which my husband never returned. Giuseppe will concur, as will each of these people." She slipped me a note with seven names upon it. I became increasingly disturbed.

"Were you not seen on the cliff path?"

"That is correct. I believe I was not seen on the cliff path. Being not seen is my specialty. But there may be some who would contest that, and say they saw me there."

I became severely uncomfortable, a state betrayed by my habit of thumping the heels of my hands together, beating but not clapping. She saw this, of course, and no doubt also observed the colour draining from my face, and the moisture starting to pustule on my brow. She cupped her hands around mine and set those exotic eyes in a bond with my fearful stare.

"I promise you, Alban, all you need to write is the truth."

"I cannot unhear what you have told me."

"And I could not conceal that from you. I revealed it as an icon of my trust."

I could see the logic and the constancy of her confession, but it did not settle my scruples. "But I am party to a slaying," I said.

"Yes," she said, and the room began to lose rigidity. My breath rattled; my pulse drummed at my temples. "You initiated the assassination with your exquisite account of our performance, but you did not intend that it would lead to so literal, and so terminal, a fall."

"I most certainly did not," I gasped.

Her hands jolted mine. "And neither did I," she beseeched.

My vision settled slightly and the hot sweat cooled. "That is not what I meant by my becoming a party to...the end. I simply meant that your confiding in me places me in a position of some professional peril."

Her grasp of my hands eased and their movement softened to a caress. "When we act without thought it could be that the lack of thought is a deception for the benefit of our conscious selves."

My rationality was regaining a foothold. "I did not act without thought," I told her. "I had been intending to elevate your worthiness for some time."

"But you did not foresee the ultimate outcome of your article."

"How could I?"

"Indeed, you could not. And neither did I. But without your viewpoint, there would not have been such bitter disagreement, and he would not have been on that cliff path in search of contentment. And his wife would not have provided him with it."

"Have you confessed this act to any other person?" I asked.

"Of course not."

Her reassurance did nothing to resolve my dilemma, and Lazuli could clearly see that my turmoil persisted. "Have you secured overnight lodgings?" she asked.

I shook my head.

"The room next to mine is vacant. Have dinner at my hotel. We can discuss it more, and in the morning, you can interview those who will buttress my testimony."

My agitation persisted, but Lazuli's touch was a type of balm I had not known, her voice seemed spherical and her spirit appeared to be floating on a wraithlike updraft. Trapped by that sensory broth, I could only comply. We finished our coffee and, linked at the elbow, she led me back to her hotel.

I could not stomach more than a bowl of soup that evening and despite her continued buoyant frame of mind, Lazuli's appetite was not significantly greater. Hence our meal lasted less than an hour. Being in the hotel dining room our conversation was conducted with discretion.

"It might be wise," I whispered, "to not appear in such good cheer."

She took my advice and before long had summoned an attitude of stifled grief. The eyes of fellow diners were thereby served with the performance they might have expected. It was during this short, but intense, conversation that Lazuli enlightened me as to her history. She was indeed from Persia. She was born close to the Caspian Sea, into a family rooted in travelling entertainment. While a child she traversed Europe performing acrobatics on the backs of ponies. It was in Vienna that she met the man we would later know as Lapis. He called himself Moritz and said he was English and Turkish, which was, she said, only half true. He was a magician with ambition, and she, aged twenty-three broke from her family and pledged herself to him. She had been happy for six or seven months, then their relationship became tempestuous, but the act was a big success and so they stayed together.

She told me some of the things Lapis had said to her. What he threatened would happen, if she compromised his career and some of his grotesque phrases.

"He would leer at me and say things like 'you will not feel my grip on your scapula' and 'you will never see the lacerations' and 'you will not feel your collarbone snap' and other threats of that nature."

"Surely you could have…"

"No, I could not. He would have found me." She brightened again. "Anyway, he was not always like that. He could be very civil, very kind. Provided the act went well and he got his encore."

"Did you remain with the same circus?"

"Not the same one. At first, we joined an Austrian one, then one from Romania, but eventually we came to England and settled with Sanger's."

"And how long with them?"

"Until…" She checked herself, I thought at first impulsively, then I considered it might be part of the grieving act, but later I would understand why. "Until – oh I don't know – around the time of the coronation. Lapis realised our act could work even better on the proscenium stage. He could command a bigger fee. He was right and became a wealthy man. For the sake of propriety, I pretended to be his wife. At least my portrayal was honest; I pretended to be respectable, while he pretended to be Persian. He bought a house." Her focus found a corner of elation. "My house."

For a shameful moment, I wondered if Lazuli's inheritance was the cause of her delight; but the certainty of it worried me. I leaned forward and whispered again. "But you are not married."

She did not bother to lower her voice. "No, I am not. But he is."

And that thought seemed to infuse her with a double satisfaction.

I took the hotel room next to the one occupied by Lazuli and awoke in the depths of that night to find her sitting on my bed.

I was sleeping naked. It was a humid night. I had thrown off the blankets and my bony frame was contoured by the single cotton sheet that separated me from her. Her hair was loose and looked much lusher and longer than I had anticipated. She wore the same blouse and brooch but her black skirt had been replaced by a brown worsted one. Her face looked older and younger than it had appeared at dinner. There were no crows' feet around the eyes, yet sacks of sadness below them. No anticipatory sparkle in her irises, but pools of interminable experience in the pupils. Gone was the excited supplication, gone was the fabricated grief, and in their place, she presented me with a sinister dolour.

"Have you ever had one of those dreams in which you know you are dreaming yet, despite all your efforts, you cannot wake up? You are your own dungeon. You are a prisoner of your sleeping self.. You might never awake."

There was a strong smell of sal volatile but that perfume deepened my immobility, almost as if to prove that I could not be revived. I saw without looking, heard without listening and tasted without touching. Was I awake? Was she? I breathed deeply not so that I might drink air, but so that I might hear its rush. I was responding, but not in the way she meant. She was talking about when a person knows they are dreaming, and I did not.

"My kiss will be a firebrand," she said, and leaned so close that her hair shuttered my perspective. I closed my eyes in anticipation, but no contact arrived. I looked again to find she was not there.

I hesitated, then scurried to the door. I was sure I had locked it. I had. It was still secured. The key was in the lock on my side. I decided that the visitation could only have been within a dream. Perhaps I was still dreaming? I doubted that, as the floorboards felt warm and I could hear distant shouts from the street intruding through the open window. I padded to it and opened it wider. There was a narrow ledge just below and I traced its line to where the next window also gaped. I would not dare to tread on it, but I had not spent my youth in a circus. I could not have left the room so silently and swiftly, but neither could I have attempted the feats I had seen Lazuli accomplish on the stage. I went back to bed, back to sleep, or back at least to dreamlessness. For a short while.

I felt her before I saw her. Her breath found me first, then a tumbling warmth from her body, then swaying tendrils of hair, a scent of lavender, a settling of her torso, the spreading of her bosom, the arch of her pubic bone. I could see only the corner of her eye, because she was kissing me.

It was serpentine and stiff, crippling and comforting, smothering and succouring, clasping and caressing, soaring and tumbling. With so little light, revelation relied on palms and fingers. Her flesh was eternal, her hair celestial, her face adorable. Her bones were possessed tracery. Her left clavicle was buckled.

I think we may have talked, but I cannot remember anything that was said. What remains melded to my soul is the calm intensity of that afterglow. I was stained glass at sunset as I subsided into glorious slumber.

My awakening was delivered by the dawn. There was a chill upon me. The bedsheet lay crumpled on the floor. I closed the window. A strand of hair, much longer than mine coiled about my hand. I dressed in a daze, frequently pausing to attempt a logical reassembly of the fractured memories of the night.

I did not see Lazuli at breakfast. I enquired at the reception counter, where they handed me a note. The clerk did not know when it had been left. Lazuli's hand comprised floral vowels and thorny consonants. She apologised for having to leave at short notice, but repeated her entreaty that I might conduct interviews with those she had nominated. She made no reference to anything that might have occurred during the night.

I was able to conduct interviews with five of the seven persons she had listed as witnesses. They did not deviate from the detail of the alibi that Lazuli had provided. Mrs Eileen White with whom she had taken tea at De Luca's, Mr Kenneth Talbot who had accompanied them back to the hotel and Royston Holdsworth the hotel porter, all confirmed the times of her whereabouts. Mrs Howson and Miss Wharton were adamant regarding seeing Mr Moritz leave the hotel alone and take the coastal path that led in the opposite direction to the De Luca Cafe. I was also able to speak to the police officer who had supervised the recovery of Moritz's corpse. It was, he said, a tragic accident. At one-thirty I went to the telegraph office to compile and dispatch my report.

I must confess that I kept a hopeful eye out for Lazuli, but she did not reappear. I returned to the hotel about three in the afternoon. I was told Mrs Moritz had left that morning while I had been in the town. My hotel bill had been settled.

My report was printed in my paper the following day. Lapis the Great had taken his final bow. Meanwhile, I assured the reader, Mrs Moritz had been taking tea with a former circus associate in De Luca's Café.

The showman's funeral was far from a private affair, though I suspect the majority of onlookers were watching in the hope of some spectacular resurrection, rather than to pay their respects. I was assigned to provide copy for my paper. The impeccably presented hearse was unintentionally reminiscent of one of Lapis's magic cabinets. The horses were jet, their plumes cobweb white. Lazuli's head was draped in a double mantilla, so dense that it might not have been her beneath it.

I was never the same after that affair. I was not of the strongest nervous disposition prior to it, but my constitution took a rattling from which it has never recuperated. I much desired to reconnect with Lazuli but good manners and poor mettle prohibited any such liaison being instigated. I busied myself with my work.

After a month of mourning, Mrs Moritz sent for me. The invitation card was edged with black. I was invited to take tea at her home in Whitebeam Avenue. As the day neared, I became wracked with apprehension. My sleep was fractured, my wakefulness restless.

It was a Sunday when Una the maid admitted me and served sandwiches and cake in the sitting room. Lazuli strode in stiffly, and still in full mourning, even to the extent of a veil of Spanish lace which she left in place throughout our hour together. She slipped her cup and her confectionary beneath the hem of the mantilla, intensifying the folds between her face and mine and further frustrating my desire to meet her eyes directly. Our intercourse was polite, careful and evasive. Neither of us hinted at any previous intimacy or confidence.

"Everything is now settled," she said.

"I am glad," I said. "There were no – complications?"

"None. I am secure. This house belongs to me. My assets are invested."

"You will not return to the stage?"

"On the contrary, I will become, I hope, invisible."

"Not entirely, I trust."

"I will not forget your assistance. I am in perpetual debt to you."

"Not so."

"Should you ever be in need of my help, Mr Graystone, you must not hesitate to request it."

Those events were the reason that, some seven months later, my brain became so overloaded that I collapsed in the Sawdoctor Street Music Hall. Lazuli's pledge was why I then fled to

Whitebeam Avenue where, after yet another diseased slumber, I collapsed once again, this time into a plate of porridge.

When Una suggested that I be given one of Lapis Moritz's shirts, the idea was so grotesque that I almost vomited. Nevertheless, there appeared no reasonable alternative. The combination of porridge, tea, honey and butter had entirely disfigured my shirt and stained my jacket. She brought the shirt, and I changed, wracked with self-consciousness, in the sitting room. I transferred the collar from my discarded shirt, and reluctantly added a tie that the maid had also brought. Meanwhile, Una managed to soften the stain on my jacket, though the lapels remained wet. I prayed that Lazuli would not be perturbed by my attire, whilst knowing that she almost certainly would.

I asked that I might apologise to Mrs Moritz, but Una regarded me as if I spoke gibberish. She reiterated that her mistress was in town, acting on my behalf. I insisted that we had spoken across the breakfast table. Una laughed, and suggested that I sat down.

The morning proceeded at a funereal rate. Several times I told Una that I should depart, but she said her mistress had forbidden it until she and I had spoken, and furthermore, I did not appear to be sufficiently well. She was right. I watched my own hands tremble. Thrice she proposed to bring more tea, but I firmly declined, terrified that I would drench my clothes again. If I stood my legs shook, when I sat my intestines rattled. The fire in the hearth offered some comfort but also laughed at me with its cackles.

It was patently evident that I could not cope with the cargo that had been loaded into my mind during the previous hours. The mix of reality, vision, dream and memory was too much and the constituent strands were too intertwined. I could not imagine a time when I might be free of this bizarre bequest. I struggled to distinguish between the superficial, the supernatural, and the infernal.

Lazuli came home at eleven thirty. I heard her being briefed by Una in mumbles suppressed by the sitting room door and by the fug of my mind. The Lazuli that entered, was once again infused with delight and encouragement.

"My dear Alban," she gushed, "pray tell me you are recovered."

"Renovated by your presence," I effused.

She looked strong, energised, mature.

"Tell me what happened."

"Another faint."

"Oh dear."

"During our conversation at breakfast."

She chuckled indulgently, smiling away my explanation. "I spoke to Cyril Chester. He will not expect you in the office today. I explained that you had been unwell last evening and were recuperating."

"What exactly did you tell him?"

"That you had collapsed at the theatre." My expression crumbled. In response she said: "I'm sure he would have heard sooner or later. Better perhaps, that it came from me."

"Did you tell him why?"

Her hesitation unsettled me. "Not in detail."

I knew at that moment that my standing at the paper would sink. I would be regarded as unwell, unreliable, fanciful and unbalanced. She overlooked my despondency and continued her lively account. "I went on to the theatre and spoke with Bob Poole at the stage door and with Miss Westhead. It was too early for Mr Crayford. No act such as you describe was seen by anyone else."

"Crayford said there had been an illusionist."

"Dicky Wren. We all know Dicky Wren. Cards and cigarettes, and cigarette cards."

I knew Dicky Wren.

"And doves with clipped wings," she added

"And gossip of my misfortune?"

She smiled and shook her head. I did not believe her. I looked at the brooch on her collar. Her lips pursed as she fixed her gaze on my throat.

"You are wearing a tie."

"Your…husband's. Also his shirt. Una brought them. I er…"

"Una explained. She is laundering your shirt."

"There is no need…"

She sat on the sofa. "Tell me what happened at breakfast."

I told her first what had, or had not, happened during the night, and how it echoed my recollection of what passed between she and I in the hotel by the coast. She reacted almost passively, but for a tightly restrained expression which edged from curiosity to recognition and on to resignation. Then I told her about the fire in the bedroom grate, the information that Una had imparted, and the discussion I thought I had had with her as she merged with the crockery, utensils and table. When I had finished, she sat almost motionless except for a slow twining of her hands. I was put in mind of one of the Fates winding a skein of destiny. She stopped, and inhaled a decision.

"Do you feel well enough to venture outside?"

We left by the rear door of the property and crossed an untended kitchen garden, and then, accompanied by the ridicule of the rooks in the whitebeams, we trampled across the saturated soil of a small field. Lazuli clutched a ring of keys. After fifty yards or so we came upon a cabin. It was secured by two locks and chains, though I doubted their necessity as the timbers were in such a poor state that a sizable screwdriver might force an entry. Inside it smelled surprisingly dry, however, and as Lazuli scraped the doors apart the purpose of the place was blatant.

"This is where we kept our properties and apparatus," she said.

I recognised immediately the horizontal and vertical cabinets that had been the focus of their greatest illusions, but it was a pair of cloth columns that demanded my attention. Each was topped by an iconic onion-shaped dome so instantly symbolic of eastern architecture. A rope stretched from each pinnacle to secure them to the cabin rafters. They must surely once have been splendid but coated in the dust of neglect they had shed their sheen. They hung like a pair of ghostly jellyfish.

"We used these in our circus days," explained my guide and almost before I saw her move, she had vanished inside one. She splayed her arms, making the spectre breathe and opening a vent to invite me in. Ensconced beside her, I recognised the warm scent of a reminiscent embrace. She shut the shroud and we could not avoid physical contact. To my surprise it was not completely dark and, following her focus, I looked up into the dome which sifted the daylight down to an almost imperceptible luminescence. She stretched on tip-toe, slightly bracing herself against me and raising her left arm. Her fingers hooked upon a bar that spanned the gape of the dome.

"In my youth," she said, "I could hoist myself inside there."

Before I could respond, she had stepped outside our sheath and swept it clear of where we stood. "And Lapis would show the whole Big Top that I was gone." She turned to face the companion drape. Meanwhile, on the other side of the ring, Livid would descend from her dome, ready to be revealed."

"Livid?"

She stroked the second silken column, careless of the decay that she disturbed on its skin. "Of course, there was a double. Of course there was..."

"A twin," I concluded.

She clutched the cloth, curling it into a fluted urn. "And there still is. And ever will be."

A draught disturbed recusant fronds of Lazuli's hair. The same essence trailed across the back of my neck. Romance and reason disputed in my brain. I felt a flush of satisfaction counterbalanced with a justified objection. "Una said there was no double."

Lazuli ignored my protest. "It was Livid who married Lapis. Those are, of course, stage names. They do not appear on the marriage certificate. English lawyers are not overly familiar with Persian forenames. So you see, there was no problem proving the marriage I never made."

The silence within the shed awaited my acceptance.

"Where is your sister now?"

Lazuli came and stood very close. She ran her fingers along the lapels of my jacket, pausing where she felt the dampness where the honey stain had been removed. She reached for my face with both hands, and for a moment I hoped she might draw my head towards her and kiss me, but instead she tapped my temples with her ring fingers. "Livid," she said, "is in here."

She then showed me the operation of the cabinets and the impossibly small spaces into which she had squeezed. To be honest, I wasn't really listening. I was more concerned with the moaning of the timbers of the cabin, which never materialised, but which I expected at every successive second. Instead of watching her demonstration I stood transfixed by the oriental fabric pillars. "Your sister," I said.

Lazuli returned to my side and regarded the second dome. "Was even more agile than I. Until she broke her collar bone."

I felt the blood sink from my cranium but breathed deeply and with a determined resolve somehow stemmed the flow. "How?"

Lazuli's face was granite. "No one knows, save her and him. But there were no teeth marks on her."

"I'm sure such an injury would not be possible by that method," I said.

"Oh it is," she said, "and was, but not at that time, and not inflicted by a human."

"What?"

Lazuli still stared at the onion dome. "Somehow her collarbone snapped. She refused to say how it had happened. Our act collapsed. You need both arms to get into there." She went to lean against the horizontal cabinet. "Sanger, the circus owner, was not happy. We were already third-rate compared to the animals and the acrobats. He put up with a reduced routine for a few weeks but cut our share of the takings and threatened to replace us. All we could do was wait. Such a fracture cannot be set. Nature has to run its course."

"How long?"

"Six weeks or more; but Livid returned sooner. Too soon. She got into that dome, but fell out. A six-foot fall onto sawdust would not normally be fatal."

"Fatal?"

"She snapped her neck."

"Dear God!"

"We left the circus."

The rooks' raucous calls rattled in the distance. The draught from the door nudged the hems of the columns. "Did it make the papers?" I asked.

"Circuses are very clever at covering up."

My professional mind would not relinquish its enquiry. "Funeral? Funeral notices?"

"Sanger's circus had Siberian tigers. Livid loved them. And vice versa."

The incredulity locked my breath.

"You must not write about this," said Lazuli. "You must tell no one what I have told you."

"Of course not," said I, hoping against hope that I could comply.

"Everything I have depends upon this great...deception."

"Yes, I can see that."

Now she did take my head in her hands. She kissed me. Not on the lips. On my forehead.

"But — the act. You moved into the music halls and the act became more spectacular than ever."

"I took on the mantle of Mrs Moritz. Lapis had the cabinets made and we began a simple concealment routine. One night, in Whitby, he failed to position them close enough. I could not switch from one to the other without being seen, and so stayed hidden. He hadn't realised and opened the door. And she stepped out."

"Your sister?"

"He didn't even realise it wasn't me, and afterwards we rowed incessantly. The only way to prove it was her was to do the same the next night with the cabinets even further apart. We could easily pass it off as a joke if it failed. It didn't fail and this time he looked more closely, and looked her in the eye. His hair turned white that week."

"And she always appeared?"

"In more and more spectacular ways."

Lazuli clasped my hands in hers and pressed her lips upon them. Then she returned to the cabinets and secured their panels shut.

"Why? Why did she do that?"

Lazuli shrugged. "She never spoke."

"She spoke to me."

"She never even glanced in the direction of her husband. But she looked at the audience, and she looked at her sister. With deep love."

"She did it for you."

"Lapis became very rich. And then..."

"He fell off the cliff."

"That was the last time I saw her. From the hotel bedroom. She was walking alongside him. On the clifftop path."

I remembered that in De Luca's café Lazuli had said that Moritz's wife had pushed him. So, I had not been covering for a killer. At least not the one I thought. There was a logic evident in what I had been told, but none of it justified my own predicament.

"So why," said I, "Is she now just appearing to me?"

"With that, I'm afraid I cannot help you," said Lazuli. "I am not my sister's keeper."

Her remark was one that I would later question.

I left in the early afternoon with my damp shirt wrapped in a linen cloth. The tram that I boarded took on the mantle of the interior of Moritz's cabinet. All the seats were taken and all the passengers were partnered by their twin, even me. Then the windows were obscured with panels slammed shut from the outside. This initiated my blue period: a state in which I remained. There should have been no light, but there was blue light. Deep blue. So deep that some folds of it were grey.

The heads of all the twins became ceramic onion domes and wobbled in synchronicity as the tram rocked along the turquoise streets and took me and my earthenware companions into the land of the livid.

By the time we reached the market square, the blue hue had dissipated. The heads of our partners fell off and rolled away. Un-twinned people disembarked and I followed, hoping for normality. I reported to the office where my colleagues greeted me with minimal sincerity. No one asked where I had been. I did no work, but stared all afternoon at the blotter on which I slowly scribbled with black ink, words that dried blue.

The shafts, beams, arcs and shadows are always blue. It is my
constant environment. It deepens and thins, but is always there. It could
be a cathedral. It is a cave. A cave without end. Labyrinthine, spherical,
intestinal, interminable.

The following day I kept normal hours. I was sent to cover court
proceedings, but to my mind the judge was a fake Persian and
Lazuli, or Livid, appeared periodically in the public gallery. The
next day I was assigned to transcribe the foreign reports, the
ones that come down the wire in cyan sparks. I made multiple
mistakes.

I went back to Whitebeam Avenue to return Moritz's shirt
and tie. Una took them. She said her mistress was not at home.
As I was leaving, I looked up at the bedrooms. One of the twins
was watching me. She did not wave.

My demeanour deteriorated; my diligence died. I worked
out my notice in a torpor. By that time, it had become my
dominant state. I was assigned menial tasks and was glad to take
them, even though I accrued mostly reprimands and derision.
The visions vested on me occurred without warning. I saw the
undead magician frequently, in the strangest of places: in the
rafters of the paper warehouse, standing in the adjacent lavatory
stall, in the stationery cupboard, in the index card drawer — yes,
a miniature Lapis: a playing card Moritz.

The handrails of the stair became sapphire serpents.
Revolving doors turned into crystal cabinets in which coats
would change colour to indigo, cobalt or ultramarine. Hats
unfurled and flapped away as enchanted carpets, spilling as they
flew, their cargo of broken collar bones, some of which were
caught in the mouths of Siberian tigers that had mutated from
lap dogs on leashes held by passing ladies who never wore blue.

The worst aspect of it all was seeing Lazuli or Livid and not being able to tell which it was. I always hoped it was the former but suspected it was always the latter. Sometimes my suspicion would be confirmed by a kinked collarbone, or a broken neck.

After my employment was terminated, I spent hours standing opposite the Moritz property in the hope that the living sister would show. She never did.

I received a letter from my bank manager and feared the worst, but to my surprise he told me that an anonymous benefactor would be making monthly deposits into my account. They were sufficient to cover my basic needs, but came with conditions. I must keep certain confidences known only to me. I must not venture along Whitebeam Avenue, nor seek to interact with any resident thereof at any other location.

Thus, my existence was prescribed. I continued to go about no business other than to await the next illusion. They came with startling invention and without warning, with unpredictable duration, never to be avoided, always shrouded in the deepest, deep blue.

I have written all this down but will not share it yet. I live in accordance with the desires of my patron. Meanwhile, the appearances continue, at least twice nightly, and also as maddening matinees. No one else ever witnesses these encounters. Lazuli was right when she said her sister now resides inside my head. Is that what spirits are? Not persons chained to places, but infections of the mind that we must carry with us wherever we go, and that cannot be purged. Has Livid shed some psychic seed in my awareness? Has her soul injected a contagion into mine?

But why? Why did she do this to me? Perhaps to set her free? For it was she who thanked me for accommodating her. It could be that, because I enabled the separation of her husband and sister, she is grateful to me. Why then torture rather than reward me? Unless, of course, the perpetrator of my pain is not she, but he.

Is Lapis my assailant? Does he want revenge for his premature retirement? Does he want me to make the ultimate report and bring retribution to his former companion? Well, it is written, but it will not be seen until long after Lazuli has exited this world.

The penultimate scenario, however, points the bony finger at my champion. The curse upon me could be the work of neither Lapis nor Livid, but the living spine of the trinity, the one I have already described as beyond human. Is Lazuli the architect of my folly? Did she select me as the draughtsman of her destiny? Did she mesmerise me into compiling the articles of her victory? Did she then cauterise my career to seal her reputation? I find this scenario too unpleasant to uphold, but too credible to disbelieve.

There is one final possibility. It is, above all others, the one that I favour. I could be my own tormentor. I can no longer distinguish between real and unreal. Maybe it was always thus? It could be that everything I have documented did not happen. I have lost the capacity to determine the difference between perception and reality and as a consequence I have become a faltering impression of my former self. I'm still here; but I have disappeared.

Regardless of who or what instigated my actions, it will be I who will conclude them. I accept all responsibility even if I am not to blame. Blame is the biggest imposter, the greatest impersonator, the showman who takes away the truth. Blame is the doppelganger of cause. It looks like the reason but, for all we know, it might just be a distraction. I have no idea how my life has played out. I do not know why I see what I see or why I do what I do. I can only report what I saw and await whatever awaits me. Meanwhile, I will continue showing up, never knowing when the next appearance will deepen my despair.

Have you ever had one of those dreams in which you know you are dreaming yet, despite all your efforts, you cannot wake up?

I have one continuously. Even when I am not asleep.

DARK WATER:
AN APPALACHIA OHIO STORY
EDWARD KARSHNER

Mount Tabor, Ohio
1921

It was past three in the afternoon when Mrs. Peabody arrived at the church in her Model T. The Reverend Richard Hanson was waiting, tea service set up in the sanctuary. He smoothed his Sunday suit, although it was Tuesday, and waited with a smile.

The Reverend Hanson watched Ella Marie Peabody walk from her automobile, carrying the strength of the hills and hollows with her. He cleared his throat and tugged his waistcoat as if to adjust a breastplate.

It was clearly established by the Apostle Paul that women should be silent and submissive in church. The authority in her presence was blasphemy. Biblical law was clear, without a husband, she should submit to the church. If the head of the celestial church was Christ, then, the head of the earthly church, this pale shadow of the one, true, divine order, was none other than The Reverend Richard Hanson.

The importance of this meeting, now, took on an ecclesiastic, if not cosmic, importance.

"Mrs. Peabody, I have a set up a tea service for us in the sanctuary," Hanson said stepping into the churchyard.

"Thank you, Reverend," she said.

There was no trace of the hollow in her voice and he wondered, how? How it was possible to physically personify one place and sound like another.

"I see you are alone. Where is your child?" He asked.

"In the care of Granny Kessler," Mrs. Peabody said.

The Reverend Richard Hanson noticed that she was sweating in the waning October sun.

"Please, come inside," he said stepping out of the way and allowing her to pass.

He followed her into the cool darkness of the sanctuary.

"Is it wise to leave a child, a baby no less, in the care of that old conjure woman?"

Mrs. Peabody removed her hat and placed it on the pew next to the table with the tea service.

"She's a granny woman. Not everyone can afford a town doctor. Even if you can, those of us out here are often considered low priority for the same economic reason. She's a friend," Mrs. Peabody said.

"Exodus 22:18, 'thou shall not suffer a witch to live'. The Bible is clear on such matters," he said.

Mrs. Peabody shot him a look that both humbled and terrified him.

"A witch?" she said. "In a hat and on a broomstick? Surely you can't be serious. And death? Death for curing rashes and hernias? What do you know of Braucherei, Reverend Hanson? Do you know that it uses the Bible for its power?"

"An abomination. The devil often hides in a sheep's skin," he said.

"And now the devil?" Mrs. Peabody said.

The Reverend Hanson started to say more – to chasten this woman who dared dismiss the power of God through the denial of the very real power of the Devil. Then he remembered what he wanted her to do.

"Tea?" he said.

"I'd prefer to handle our business quickly so I can get home before hollow dark."

"Yes, of course," he motioned for her to sit.

"As you are aware, I'm sure," Mrs. Peabody started, "with the deaths of my husband and my parents, I've decided to leave the hollow and return to Atwater."

Reverend Hanson folded his hands in his lap.

"I am prepared to settle the matter of the church lease as was determined by my father," Mrs. Peabody pulled a bank folder from her large leather bag and placed it on the table.

"Within, Reverend Hanson, you will find the original agreement made by my father to the founding church community. My understanding..." she started.

The Reverend Richard Hanson fought the urge to roll his eyes so hard that a pain shot down his face. The false modesty of this one, this serpent, did not suit her. My understanding, he mocked her practiced mid-Atlantic accent in his head. She understood perfectly.

"My understanding is that the graveyard will revert to the church as a donation along with the adjacent grounds that run to the creek. That land, now consecrated, is to remain a graveyard. However, the land upon which the church sits, as well as the parsonage and common grounds can be purchased or leased at the original agreed upon sum," Mrs. Peabody folded her hands.

The Reverend Hanson removed the documents from the folder and glanced at them. There was the transfer deed for the graveyard. Then, the purchase agreement for the church and the land itself. He smiled politely and placed the documents back in the folder.

"I'll be happy to discuss these with your lawyer or your banker. Thank you for bringing them," he said.

"You may discuss them with me. This is my land and my business," she said.

Hanson smiled. "Your father's land and business."

"He's dead."

"Then, your husband."

Mrs. Peabody didn't pause.

She said, "Also dead."

There. She had followed his logic with perfection and trapped herself within the syllogism.

"Then, Mrs. Peabody, it appears that with both your father and husband deceased, your business becomes the business of the church. So, I'll have the Pastor Parish committee draw up a full transfer deed for your signature," he said.

She said, "That is completely unacceptable."

"Mrs. Peabody, this is the Lord's home. We must remain respectful," he said.

Mrs. Peabody picked up her bag.

"It may be the Lord's home, but it is on my land. Land you will either purchase, lease, or remove yourself. I'll leave those papers with you. I know the Pastor-Parish Committee meets tomorrow. I'll see you Thursday for your decision," she said.

"Please, Mrs. Peabody, you are hysterical with grief. Come sit. Have another cup of tea and be reasonable," Hanson said.

Mrs. Peabody started down the aisle toward the door.

"You can sign them or not. That is up to you," the mid-Atlantic accent was strangled out as her Hillican accent regaining its authority. "Either way, you can go piss up a rope, you pompous toad."

He watched her leave the sanctuary and heard the Model T sputter to life. Hanson grabbed the folder and beat it on the table until his teacup spilled over. The tea ran over the table and pooled brown on the thick folder. He grabbed the cup and threw it watching with release as it shattered against the wooden cross above the altar.

"You are a goddamned witch!" Hanson yelled to the voided sanctuary.

*

Timothy Buxton, esquire, pulled on his beard and pushed the paper back to Reverend Richard Hanson.

"These documents are legal and in order. I suggest the lease. It would be what is best for the church now and offers the most possibilities for the future," Buxton said.

Reverend Hanson sat at the head of the long table in the fellowship hall. The faces of the ten men looked at him. Waiting to see how he would react to Buxton's legal opinion.

"With all due respect, Mr. Buxton, that is not how Biblical law works. Traditionally, once the men have passed, the church becomes the custodian of property. One should not have to ask for what is already theirs," Reverend Hanson said.

Buxton crossed his arms and leaned back in his chair.

"With all due respect, Pastor, we ain't in the Bible. This is Kinnikinnick County and the law says you can't force someone to give you something. That'll be called theft," Buxton said.

Hanson frowned. Buxton was the only parishioner to not address him as 'Reverend'. It had been an early sore spot. Hanson had insisted and Buxton had replied that no man was to be 'revered'. It wasn't 'usual', he said.

"Maybe she can be reasoned with? If enough of us go to talk with her," Tim Schlep said.

Hanson welcomed a debate that removed him from the centre.

"Reasoned to what end?" Buxton said. "This land is hers. The agreement is one we've all been aware of since her Daddy signed the papers years back. Not a one of us would be doing things differently should we be in her position."

"Except," Hanson started.

"There is that, Tim. I mean, she's a girl," Steve Bascomb finished.

"It doesn't matter. The agreement was with her Daddy and this body. Still is. She is the executer of that agreement, now. What she's got going on under her clothes isn't of issue," Buxton said.

Hanson leaned forward. "Except, the Bible says otherwise. Her true Father still lives and therefore holds this agreement."

Buxton laughed. "Good luck making that argument in court."

The room quieted. There was an electricity that worked its way between the seated members. Hanson could feel it. Despite Buxton's attempt to make this issue one of secular law, Hanson could tell there was a desire to settle this issue with Biblical law. To do otherwise would render all of this, this building, this land, the spiritual wellness of these people a sickly, desiccated waste.

"I have prayed over this matter and, to be honest, my meeting with Mrs. Peabody has deepened my fears," Hanson said.

The room hummed with anticipation and Hanson let it simmer to the point of boiling over.

"Mrs. Peabody may not be in her right mind," Hanson said.

Buxton said, "Because she won't sign over her land to you? That doesn't make her crazy. That makes her practical."

"I didn't say crazy. I fear she has been bewitched," Hanson said.

Everyone around the table sat up, except Buxton. He folded his arms tighter and let loose a long sigh.

"After the passing of Mr. Peabody, it came to my attention that, in her grief, she began to seek the council of the old Kessler woman who lives at the end of the hollow," Hanson said.

The committee members leaned forward.

"Last evening, she mentioned the conjure woman with such reverence that it made me fear for her child who was left in the old crone's care," Hanson said.

"Pastor, that woman delivered the child of every man on this board. She's also fixed us up from scrapes and bumps. Staunched our blood when we've been cut. She's nothing to be afraid of," Buxton said.

The men at the table stared at their hands.

"Healed you? And yet, does not the scripture say that only Jesus Christ can heal? Is she Jesus Christ?" Hanson said.

"Actually, pastor, the Good Book, Acts in particular, says Jesus gives his disciples the power to cure in his name. Those of you in here who have been healed by Granny Kessler know that is exactly what she does. Nothing she does is outside the Bible," Buxton said.

Hanson clinched his fist.

"Then why does she hide in the hills? Why conceal this power? See? I am here. Where I can be found. Why does she separate herself from a community you say she serves," Hanson said.

"She's a Hillican. That's where they like to be. In the hills," Buxton said.

Hanson smiled. You couldn't obscure the self-evident with logic. This matter required eloquence.

"As I have prayed on this matter, I have come to the conclusion that this conjure woman is set to destroy us, this town, one soul at a time," Hanson said.

As the committee exchanged looks, Buxton leaned even further back until his chair rocked and creaked. He ran his fingers through his hair.

"Please," Buxton said.

"Each person that seeks her aid, each one who goes up alone, is a lost sheep she peels from the flock. Slowly, she siphons souls for her true master," Hanson preached.

The men looked at each other. They thought. Skepticism slowly giving way to fear. Need.

"Once, when I was there for some foot cream, I seen that she had a shelf of empty jars. Asked me to sit in a chair before them," Tom Wilcox said.

The men at the table murmured.

"Jesus, Tom. I bet you go up there now and those jars are full of chowchow, corn, and pickles," Buxton said.

"Do not blaspheme in this house," The Reverend Hanson said.

Buxton stood up and looked each man at the table in the eye.

"I won't entertain this foolishness a minute longer," Buxton said. He set his eyes on Hanson. "Take the lease. Sign it. That's my legal advice. Personally, I have an idea what you're up to. So, watch yourself. I'll be watching you."

The men at the table shifted uncomfortably as Buxton walked from the room. Then, they looked at the Reverend Hanson.

"What'll we do, Reverend?" Steve Bascomb said.

This had gone better than he expected. So, well, in fact, he had not anticipated needing an end play. So, he let the drama stay in motion.

"Go home and pray. Tomorrow, I shall meet with Mrs. Peabody. At that time, all will be revealed. I anticipate an acceptable conclusion to this matter," Hanson said.

The men nodded in agreement.

Hanson looked at his assembled flock. As long as there were men needing to be led, there would be leaders of men. He pulled their anxiety to him with relish.

*

In the beginning, God separated the waters above from the waters below and held them in their place with a firmament, a vault, allowing the Earth to emerge. From the void, the Lord created space. It was this space, in the between, where humans thrive as the caretakers of the Made.

However, the spirit of man was corrupted with the forbidden teachings of the Fallen Ones. The Lord grieved. His spirit no longer dwelt among them. So, what was done? The Lord opened the vaults. It wasn't merely a flood. The water above reunited with the water below. Noah did not merely float over a flooded earth. He sailed his boat over the dark, watery void that preceded creation itself. He was an old man in a new world. A world made new by the collapse of the firmament.

As the rain came down in sheets and the creek rose, Hanson had little doubt that the end of the old and the start of the new was upon him. He was the new Noah. The church his ark. He remembered as he slipped in the mud, his burden heavy, the purpose of the flood was not to save Noah; rather, it was to eradicate the evil that threatened Noah's walk with God. Christ the Savior also took up this teaching. Better to remove the offending limb than have it rot the whole body.

Victim. From the Latin victima meaning a creature killed as a religious sacrifice. Those who the flood took away, were victims as sacrifice. A way to cleanse and feed the new world that was set to emerge. Noah was no murderer for his part. He was the first priest of the new temple. Protecting the spiritual life of the chosen through the ritual slaughter of the wicked.

Hanson tossed the rope up over the branch he could see through the undulating, liquid dark. There is but one order. All others are a crooked path. He pulled. He fell. He screamed but climbed back up using the oak tree for support. He pulled again. The burden lifted. He would not only walk the straight path he would straighten the crooked one. He pulled again and the burden rose higher, the rain lubricating the soft bark of the limb. Pieces of tree pelted his face like buckshot with each successful pull.

The victim swung, freely relieved of life and gravity. A sacrifice to the rain and the dark waters that rose from below, freed from their vault. He tied the end of the rope to the hitching post and fell to his knees.

It was finished.

His eyes burned as the light found them and he closed them. His mind was quiet. His ears heard only the slap of rain around him. Then...

"Reverend Hanson, what's happened?" Steve Bascomb said over the pounding and rushing water.

Hanson opened his eyes to see the chosen flock. Some had gathered around the swinging body of Ella Marie Peabody.

"She has given herself to the dark one. I couldn't stop her," Hanson said.

"The child? Where's the child?" It was a female voice Hanson could not place.

He looked over his shoulder at Esau Creek.

"Thrown into the water. Given to that which lies beneath the firmament," he said. Then he collapsed.

*

Mount Tabor
1925

The water had turned, again. The little boy who sat on the old well cap had told him it would. Three wells. Each one quickly soured with a smell that rose from the ground and hung in the air like a tattered shroud. All the water, it seemed, had gone bad. After the second well, he'd asked parishioners to bring him water from their wells. From their homes.

To be of service to the shepherd of the Lord, they had complied in numbers. Cases of glass jars filled with the sweet water from hidden streams, seeps, and deep cold wells that taped into the ancient Tayes River. But, within an hour, the clear water turned brown, muddy, taking on a smell of Sulphur and old meat. It teemed with worms and beetles.

Hanson had even gone into town. He thought the city water in Atwater would be better. Cleaner. Treated and safe unlike the natural water that came from the ground. It too, soured once it was in the parsonage. He could still smell the chlorine. But the foul creatures who swam within the glass jug seemed unbothered by the purifying effects of modern chemical treatments.

He studied his books and THE Book. His thirst growing harsher day by day. He could feel his eyes and his brain drying. His hands were beginning to take on the look of a brown paper sack. His skin stretched tight over bone like parchment paper. He was wasting.

The boy who sat on the well watched.

Those evening ambulations the Reverend Hanson was known for, stopped. He could no longer meander in meditative bliss under the severe countenance of the boy.

Hanson concluded that it was the Deep causing his suffering. He was being tormented by that primordial evil the Lord had trampled down so His order could emerge. Yet, it was still there. Dormant, waiting.

It occurred to Hanson that this place, so blessed with water, might be cursed. That all the streams, creeks, runs, seeps, springs, ponds were just cracks in the firmament where the ancient evil bubbled out. That it wasn't just the water that was sour but the entirety of the land itself. All of it cursed.

And that explained so much. How could these people drink the water? How could they not smell the foulness of it? Choke on the acrid taste of it? Because they were already infected by it.

He prayed in the parsonage. But he could hear the boy scratching and milling around. He moved to the church and prayed so often there that he started sleeping in the sanctuary where the boy could not come. Could not spy on him or listen.

And his thirst seemed to grow with the putrification of the water. Then it came to him in the depth of prayer. The sky above. That was the domain of the Lord. The water that fell from heaven, like mana, was from the Lord. He would collect rainwater. The purest of all water. The holiest water that was squeezed from Heaven itself.

He cleaned and arranged pots and pans to collect that water that would finally heal him and restore his vigor for what would come.

Then, the drought came.

*

Mount Tabor
1934

Orchard Hill stood sentinel at the end of Thurston Hollow. It had always been a wild place. Home to horse thieves and bootleggers. Now, nearly all of Orchard Hill was in the process of being made a state park. But for one eighty-acre section. That was the home of Eunice Kessler. The last legal inhabitant of Orchard Hill. Through fear, stubbornness, and, some said, magic, she remained. Alone.

The Reverend Richard Hanson parked his city car at the base of the hill near the trail that wound itself through the trees to her homesite. He followed the switchbacks that rose five-hundred feet in less than a quarter mile.

He leaned against an oak tree and looked at the trail ahead that was nearly vertical.

"How does an old woman do this?"

Pulling himself up from sapling to sapling, finding foot holds in tree roots, Hanson reached the top and sucked in the pungent air of the woods. Through a break in the tangle of maple and white mulberry, he saw a glimpse of the Kinnikinnick River Valley below. Green, alive. The twisted blue of the river cutting through the middle. He looked to his right where the trail led and pushed on.

The woods opened to a clearing that sat at the highest point. On either side of the path were stretches of gardens. Late vegetables and herbs. Flowers. Hollyhocks and sunflowers waved in the breeze, serving as climbing cages for beans. Where the path continued past the gardens, the trees started again. Apples and peaches. Pawpaws. There, almost hidden by the forest that continued beyond, was a small house made of thick oak beams.

He stopped. There at the threshold, a basket in hand, was the witch of Orchard Hill.

Younger than he expected – she was probably the same age as he was, late thirties. Tall and thin, but strongly built. She was wearing a blue work dress and had a flowered scarf tied around her head. The woman placed the basket on the doorstep and walked forward.

Hanson froze.

She stopped where the garden started.

"What brings you all the way up here, mister?" she said.

Hanson swallowed.

"I'm the Reverend Richard Hanson, pastor of Mount Tabor Community Church."

"I'm Eunice. Folks call me Granny Kessler. This is my hill," she said.

They looked at each other as the wind rustled in the treetops, whispering so as to listen.

"I'm in need of help," he said. "I fear I am close to death."

She took three long strides toward him and stopped.

"Not yet," she said looking at him. She took in a deep breath. "But you's as dried up as a string of leather britches."

"I'm thirsty. Yet I cannot drink," he said.

"What've you lived on, then?" She asked.

Hanson swallowed. His sore throat shredded his words.

"Beer. Sometimes liquor. I drink what I can until it sickens me," Hanson said.

"Let's have a look at you then." Granny Kessler took his arm and led him toward the house.

She put him in a chair on the porch and handed him a mason jar of water with crushed mint. He drank deeply. It was water. Pure water. It was cold. Clean. He took another drink looking at the pitcher full of spring water on the table.

She sat across from him with her own jar of water. She was peeling a small green apple with a pen knife.

"You seem to be drinking fine, now," she said.

Hanson finished the jar.

"May I have more?" He said.

"Help yourself," she said.

"Is this witchcraft? The water?" he said.

"It's just water," she said.

"Water, down there, in Mount Tabor and even in Atwater, is sour. It goes bad. Creatures breed in it. Undrinkable," he drank and felt the cool water and mint ease his throat.

She put the knife down and offered him half an apple. He took it.

"Shouldn't be that way. The water all through this county is sweet water. Best water in the world. The Tayes runs right through there." She started to gently rock in her chair. "Is it a problem for everybody?"

Hanson swallowed and looked at the jar. She nodded and he poured another jar full.

"It appears to be just me," he said.

She pulled her chair closer.

"Put your jar down," she said.

He did and she took his hands and squeezed them. Her fingers squeezed between bone and muscle. He winced but sat still.

"Water is a funny thing. The old ones, the Shawnee and those what lived here before them, figured water to be the earth's blood. Others, our people, figure water to be more alive. To be memory. Or more like dreams. But water holds everything. That Tayes River? It's as old as the dinosaurs. It remembers them. It remembers all that come after. It knows us now and will hold memories of us when we go," she said.

He wanted to pull his hand away but couldn't. He wanted to take her water but was afraid to move.

"Your church, the one that's on Essau Creek?" she said.

He nodded.

"That's a funny place. Lots to remember there. My husband said it was a haunted place. A place best forgotten," she said letting go of his hands.

"When did this start? How long?"

Hanson thought about that night, nearly fifteen years ago in the rain. The storm. The battle at the creek. The sacrifice made.

He said, "A while. It seems to progress. At first it was only the well at the parsonage. I thought the boy at the well had done something to the well. A prank if you will. But..."

"Boy at the well?" she said.

"Yes. I don't know who he is."

Granny Kessler started rocking. "When?"

"Pardon?"

"When? Does he sit in the day? Of an evening?" she said.

Hanson thought.

"Just after sunset. He sits there until morning," Hanson said.

"What did you stir up down there?"

Hanson swallowed. The dryness to his throat returned.

"I'm not sure I know what you mean," he said.

She pointed to the jar of water next to him.

"Have a drink," she said. "You're parched."

He took the jar. The smell hit his nose before the water his lips. Like a spoiled potato. It had turned cloudy red. Hanson let go of the jar and it shattered on the porch. Insects scattered from the broken glass to the shelter under the plank boards.

"What did you do?" he said trying to stand.

"Me? That's your water," she said.

Hanson's hands trembled. The precious water he had finally drank now poured out of him as sweat.

"What is it you don't want to remember? What is it the land needs you to remember?"

"Land isn't sentient. I am its master," he said.

She rocked slowly.

"And yet it's a'killing you and you won't take notice," she said.

He stared at his feet wanting to avoid her eyes.

"As I said, the land there has always been uneasy. You brought all them nasties to the surface. It don't want to hurt you. It wants you to make amends," she said.

"Amend? The land does not speak. It demands nothing."

"'Now art thou cursed from the earth, which hath opened her mouth to receive thy brother's blood from thy hand.' Ain't that right? Who does the cursing? The earth speaks for herself," she said.

Hanson tried to stand but was too weak.

"I can fix you, some."

"Fix me how?"

"I can staunch it. Make it so you can drink. It won't last," she said. "It ain't a cure."

"How long?" If only he could get his strength back, be able to travel. He could flee this cursed land. Return to northern Ohio, civilization, urban modernization. Be free from all this regressive hocus pocus.

"Long enough to set whatever you done right," she said.

"If I've done nothing?"

She leaned forward.

"The land and water say otherwise. You are as full of those nasties as the water. It's you who are cursed not the land," she said.

Hanson tried to move his chair back. "Can you read minds?"

She laughed. "I don't need to. I know men."

He could feel his throat tighten and his tongue stick to his teeth. Her jar of clear spring water, mint leaves settled to the bottom, sat on the ground next to the old woman. It was pure because it was not his. He felt himself getting angry.

"Do your witchery. I'm beyond my capacity to endure the suffering."

She built a fire of seasoned oak and ash in a fire pit between the gardens and the house. From inside, she fetched a toolbox and sat it on the ground by the fire that seemed to burn invisible, but hot, in the shank of day.

"Come here," she said.

Hanson pushed himself out of the chair and walked carefully toward the fire. The ground was uneven, and his legs unsteady.

She put her hands on his shoulders and positioned him with his back to the sun.

"Stand here as such," she said.

"Why?"

"I'm fixing to do you a need of work."

From the toolbox, she took a spool of red string. She measured it from the top of his head to the tip of his toes and cut it with a pair of shears. Then, she measured his head like a haberdasher and tied a knot in the sting.

She said, "O Lord my God, I cried out to you, and you healed me."

Granny Kessler wrapped the string around the circumference of his chest, tied a knot and said "O Lord my God, I cried out to you, and you healed me."

Then, she measured each arm, tying a knot for each and said, "O Lord my God, I cried out to you, and you healed me."

She stepped back and began to wind the thread in her hand.

"Why do you quote scripture to do witchcraft?"

"Honey, this ain't witchcraft. It's healing. All healing comes from Jesus Christ. Don't you know that?"

This was a trick. It had to be. A way to further his suffering.

She walked to the fire and held the string over it. She closed her eyes and took in a long breath.

"Our Lord God went to a field, on a Gods-Acre, He plowed three furrows, he found three worms. The one is white, the other is red, the third is death for all ye worms. In the Three Highest Names," she said, dropping the string in the fire.

It flared up and Hanson felt his thirst vanish. His throat was cool and his mouth no longer felt like burnt cotton.

"How?" he said. "How did you do that?"

"I didn't. T'was the Lord," she said. She crouched at the toolbox and closed it. "But, like I said, it ain't no cure. Remember the words, Psalms 30, you have to cry out to the Lord. That's the only way for you to get fixed."

She walked to the porch, and he followed with new energy.

"No. No. If you can do this, you can finish it. You can make me whole again," Hanson said.

"I ain't the one what broke you. Whatever you did, and I got a notion, you need to pray on it and fix it. Then, you can be made whole. I just helped you get your body straight to purify your conscience," she said.

"Bullshit," he reached for her arm.

She pushed the palm of her hand into his chest hard enough to knock him off the porch. Granny Kessler held up a finger.

"Seek to put hands on me again and you'll wish thirst was your only problem," she said.

He pulled himself up.

She filled six mason jars with the mint water from the pitcher.

"These will stay until the next new moon. In that time, you need to do right by those you wronged. You might think they's gone. That they can't get you. But they's gonna wring the life out of you until you fix this."

Hanson took the box of mason jars.

"I still have no idea what you are talking about," he said.

"Then, you'll dry up like an old cow turd and another will have to fix your mess," she said.

He started to deny his sin again and she held up her hand.

"I'm done with you. I tried to help. You know what you need to do. Now git. Git before I end your suffering for good."

Hanson smirked and felt the weight of the water.

"I don't believe in throwing hexes, you old witch," he said.

She reached behind the door and took out her Sears and Roebuck 12-gauge side by side. She put the stock under her arm, the barrel hovered steadily at his feet.

"I told you, I got no need or use for witchcraft. Especially not to handle a weak-backed peckerwood such as yourself. Now, git," she said.

Hanson made for the trail between the gardens listening to the clink and jingle of his magic witch water. One week. He had one week before the new moon. One week to get himself better and free of this place. His legs found new energy as he descended the trail to his city car. She would be the one who would be sorry. It would be her who would pay.

By the time he made it to his car, the sun had been blotted out by the squat foothills of the Appalachian plateau plunging the hollow into the gloaming. His foot caught on a gnarled tree root and his ankle twisted sending him sprawling onto the gravel road. On his stomach, his face bruised, he watched the jars tumble through the air then shatter on the ground with the rhythm of gunfire. He crawled forward.

"No. No, please," he buried his face into the ground and chewed the mud. "Please God, why?"

He knew why. He only hoped that God would not see the lie. If God really existed at all.

*

Mount Tabor
1934

The Reverend Hanson pondered the power of a week as he tried to discern the silhouette of the new moon obscured to a smear by the canopy of ash and oak trees. It wouldn't be long, now.

In his struggle against those watery forces that would undo his church and, thereby, his community, he had been grievously wounded. His eyes were sunken and yellow, teeth turned brown. Dried spittle clung to his lips. Each day he wasted more into nothing. Hanson stared at his dry, cracked hands. His nails long and chipped. He was becoming something else. Or nothing else at all.

And he was alone. Except for the boy who was back at the well. The lad's legs dangled over the cap and they swung to the rhythm of the tune he was whistling.

"Boy," Hanson said, "what song are you whistling, there?" His voice was weak and reedy.

The boy stopped, looked at Hanson. A grin spread across his face.

Hanson pulled himself as straight as he could.

"How dare you demean the battles I have fought for this community. I am a soldier against evil. There is no mercy for those who stand against the will of the Lord," Hanson said.

The boy started to whistle again.

Hanson could feel the water below churn and roll. His ears buzzed. The rancid cider and beer he'd lived on began to claw its way up his throat. If the battle was to be fought, he would choose the field. He entered his church and locked himself in the sanctuary.

He huddled against the chancel listening to the thick sloshes as it slapped itself against the sacristy. The wet seeped up from below. The knees of his trousers saturated.

"I was your man," he screamed at the empty cross above the alter. "Your agent."

He fell back into the turbid churn that was slowly pulling him apart.

"Even now, will you not stand with me? Stand with me against the dark forces that come for us?" Hanson said.

He was alone, still – dissolving, being incorporated into the fluid agitation of...

It wasn't God. It wasn't the devil or witches. It was what was in him.

The dark water had come to claim its own.

A RESPECTABLE TENANCY
ROSE BIGGIN

From: tobiasm@branchoutestates.org
To: jeremyf@branchoutestates.org
11/10/2024 16.47
Fwd: those Greenwood Grounds letters

Hiya J,

As requested – here are the docs me and Ann told you about at B's drinks, the ones rolled up in the old title deed/whatevr it was.

Would have the intern type it all up instead of poor Ann pulling an all-nighter but I'm not risking anything getting out before we've had chance to further discuss so please mind any typos/etc.

Let me know what you think??? Possible angle for us? historical precedent...? Natch would need to check with legal etc to iron out details, potential risks etc. But could be effective – not part of our official agreements/contracts ofc! just something we could float, mention it if we need, potential leverage sort of thing if there's any clients claiming issues of cashflow/ crisis/disruptoin etc - and if we're only talking single digits anyway?

Let me know
Best
Toby

Tobias Marston
Senior Partner & Co-CEO, Branching Out Estates
"Real Results"

Forwarded Message:

From: annak-w@branchoutestates.org
To: tobiasm@branchoutestates.org
Date: 11/10/2024 09.22
Subject: those Greenwood Grounds letters

Hi T

working from home today at least til lunch-ish because im knackered, had to spend half the night trying to decode these things before I could even start typing the handwriting gets SO BAD by the end – but here we go. finally got it done, here they are, see attached. you owe me at least the next round, okay? or two

Annnnnnnnnnnnnnn(other round after that)

Anna Kirkleigh-Winter
Branching Out Estates
"Real Results"

Attached documents (14):

(1)

Oakbeam House
Greenwood Grounds,
near Kent.
May 10th, 1844.

Dear Mother,

How excited I am to write to you from our new home, which I can say, truthfully and meaning it, 'tis an accurate statement to say: I am currently sitting at a writing-desk in our new house, which is, yes, in the midst of the (fabled!) estate of Greenwood Grounds! We have done it!

I am aware you have not heard from me for some time while this move has been taking place and I apologise for the worry this must have caused you and Father. Please excuse the delay in this missive and know you have been constantly in my thoughts. The truth is that I did not wish to write until we were finally in and settled, and there has been so much to do in the arrangements and continued preparations for upheaving our whole brood up and across the country to Greenwood – how is it that each task when one is moving house becomes a cursed box that opens out to reveal two, three, four dozen more tasks? – but, now, just as Spring is upon us, we finally find ourselves safely lodged in our new house. We live in Greenwood, Mother!

Let me assure you: life here is as pleasant as we were hoping it would be. Even more so, perhaps. From the moment we stood in the doorway we felt completely at home.

The entry hall is a wonder, welcoming you with the imposing sight of the chandelier that comes down low on a big chain to illuminate the sweeping staircase. It is all exactly as you'd imagine, as you would wish. As for our room...! The headboard is finely carved in dark oak and the bed is the comfiest thing I have ever made contact with. I must also tell you the breakfast room had the most darling porcelain set in blue and white and so for the time being I am going to leave our older set wrapped in tissue paper, it seems sensible to preserve your generous wedding present. (Speaking of which: Matthew sends his regards and love, of course!)

Oakbeam House is one of the largest medium-sized properties in Greenwood and its land stretches to fully six acres, with considerable forestry on the westernmost side. There is a greenhouse too, and Johnson has assured me the production of vegetables for pickling and the orchard for which to bring forth our own jams will be a smooth operation. I am excited for all of us to settle into this bucolic life, after so much stress in the town. Truly, Mother, I cannot comprehend how blessed we are to have secured a Greenwood property. For all the talk of the peculiar rental situation (and I will admit it is idiosyncratic), it is a competitive process to be here, and besides, now we are here, it doesn't seem so bad. In any case, eight years is a great many years away so no need to be thinking about that just yet.

The children love it – the eldest four, especially, are beyond delighted to have rooms of their own. As for the others, Crabbe is busy painting the nursery-room as I write, and I have already set up three neat little crib beds. In fact, I must go and advise him to try to have that finished before Matthew returns so he will not be disturbed by the smell of paint (he is out securing some of the final bits of paperwork).

I remain,
Your ever-loving daughter,
Eveline

(2)

Oakbeam House,
June 8th, 1850

Mother,

Life passes in bliss here at Greenwood. If I close my eyes, a flickering shadowplay of the time: the children playing in the orchard, racing to touch each tree and back, growing older, yes, but never losing their childlike joy in life; taking family walks along the river and down to the fields; blissful mornings of silence in the breakfast room; Matthew and I reading by the fire...

We are aware the rent is coming due and Matthew and I have been in discussions of how to manage it. We still have some time, of course, and I am not worried, only aware that what is still a few years hence at the moment will soon be upon us, and we don't wish to be caught unprepared or unawares.

It helps that we get on so well with some of the neighbours! The Fortunes in particular have been great friends and good advisors. We met in our first months at Oakbeam House and have called upon each other often since. They have fewer children than us; only five.

The Fortunes have lived in Greenwood for two rounds of rent before us. Mrs Tilda Fortune is a kind and intelligent woman; we have spent many a pleasant afternoon together. She has a keen interest in embroidery, in fact she has promised next season to reupholster our ottoman! Naturally this prompted me to ask the obvious; in response she claims she is as good with the needle as she ever was. Still, the sight is one to get used to, and prompted Matthew to decide he shall take responsibility for the first rent – since he has also managed so much of the paperwork for our coming to Greenwood, perhaps he feels in some way it is his duty. I told him we have plenty of time to finalise details of the arrangement and not to think about it too much yet.

Your daughter
Eveline

(3)

Oakbeam House
April 2nd, 1852

Mother,

I recall writing to you to say rent would soon be upon us — how blissfully in the past that feeling seems now, for, in truth, we still had a while to go! Now the day is fast approaching — and indeed it is to be measured in days, not months nor years not even weeks — I confess I feel a dreadful anticipation and wish I had again the happiness of it being a few years off. When I look around at the dining-room with its beautiful varnished table or stand atop the staircase in the main hall and admire the portraits along the wall, it is very nice, but I almost think such pleasures are not to be acquired for such a rent as this. Tilda Fortune has been visiting to reassure me but her presence, I confess, only makes me more concerned for surely it should be I, not Matthew...! But he is insisting. We had the most fraught discussion the other night, the tension had been simmering all week but he told me we had both accepted to the terms upon moving in and there was no use crying about it now. This only aggravated my upset, and I threatened to fling the soup tureen out of the attic-room window (we had run up there for privacy it being the furthest point from the servants' quarters and the hearing of the children) – not to damage the tureen but just to make some great crashing loud noise that might express my unhappiness.

But it is decided: Matthew leaves the day after tomorrow, first thing in the morning: truthfully, I do not know how I will manage to get through such a great yawning stretch of hours before then, and as for once he is away...! The children are aware of what is happening but do not feel, as I do, the same sense of dread, I think it is not quite real to them.

I shall write again once the event has passed.

All my love,
Your Eveline

(4)

Oakbeam House
April 15th, 1852

Mother,

You cannot imagine the embarrassment I feel at the display of upset in my previous letter. I can only hope it did not cause you much anguish; rest assured the emotions it describes are obsolete, and you may disregard its sentiments. For Matthew has come home with the rent duly paid, and truthfully there is barely any difference. The children might not have even noticed it if he hadn't shown them; and, I dare say, perhaps I wouldn't have either.

He spoke of the landlord (one Mr Edward Booth is currently running things in Greenwood) as the very model of friendliness, a stout fellow in a frock coat with fine buttons, who opened the door himself before showing Matthew through into a back-room done up tastefully with potted ferns, clapping him on the back with a hearty smile and offering a glass of brandy.

The brandy was medicinal, of course, not only a matter of polite hospitality, and Matthew quickly realised this, so he told me. But he did not mind, in fact if anything he approved; and this, it turned out, was not the only thoughtful preparation to be made.

The first glass of brandy duly dispatched, and a second offered and poured, the Landlord (for so everyone calls him; Mr Booth is simply the current iteration, you see, Greenwood is established enough that generations have passed in his position) – the Landlord rung a bell which summoned a neat fellow in a starched apron carrying a small carpet-bag. He introduced this fellow as his personal doctor who would be performing the procedure. So, all the more reason not to worry! For it was done with a professional air and Matthew's own comfort was the highest priority.

The Landlord excused himself and it took place there in the parlour.

The doctor administered a tincture and an injection which knocked Matthew out; apparently the amputation took less than a minute because of his expertise with the saw (which was a tiny thing, Matthew said; barely more than a butter knife with ambition, really) and the delicateness of the bone. When Matthew came to, his hand had been carefully bandaged, and he was given a set of bottles containing pills for the recurrent pain, which will fade before too long in any case.

The children are morbidly fascinated by the sight of Matthew's hand without its little finger. I have touched its former place delicately and I cannot deny how strange it is. He is taking it in high spirits and after all, it being his weakest hand as well, it is hardly affecting his daily activities, he says.

And now we can look into a bright future of eight more years at Greenwood (and in fact I believe the future will be brighter for longer than that, since it can only be easier from now on, now the worst is known, if worst is even the word!)

Yours in relief and love,
E

(5)

Oakbeam House,
Greenwood
October 23rd, 1854

Mother,

Autumn is such a beautiful season. Matthew and I have begun to make a habit of an early morning constitutional (sometimes we manage it before the children are awake!) — we walk arm-in-arm along the sweeping pathways and watch the mists rising over the trees in their idyllic dapples of russets, golds, bronze. Splotches of black upon the beeches, their papery leaves like thousands of yellow coins!

You'll be pleased to hear how well we are getting on. Matthew and I are truly best friends at the moment. I know I have a palpable glow about me, not only due to my condition, although that is the source of much joy too, of course. Tilda says we might keep fingers crossed for twins!

Perhaps we can discuss yourself and father coming to visit?

Your daughter,
Eveline

(6)

Oakbeam House,
Greenwood
February 18th 1860

Mother,

It is that time again — how does it go by so quickly? — when the lake is crackling over with a thin sheet of ice and the night falls swiftly into darkness.

We fell into some argument during dinner last night; but it was not as difficult as it might have been, considering the subject: that our next rent is coming due. Hard to believe where the time goes; but those darling children who used to bounce and caper so happily through the leaves are older now, they are mature enough to understand the arrangement and be involved in the conversation and decision. My stomach grew tight in anticipation of a bitter argument but, in the end, it was easily resolved. Benson is old enough to appreciate what living in Greenwood has done for him and he is mature enough, now his six years are fourteen, to understand the implications. Sheila sulked for a while; I think she wanted to volunteer first but the two of them did not argue, which was a relief, and anyway she is a year younger than Benson, and it is very important to Matthew and I that the children are mature enough to understand the undertaking if and when they undertake it. We would never foist it upon anyone or simply order what we have decided — as we have heard that ghastly patriarch of the Campbells does, over in East Greenwood! and a servant is hardly fair, we'd never do that; it must be voluntary, this is of prime importance to us — so, we have as a group decided upon Benson's little toe. Best get it over with and I can start getting used to it, he said, looking about the dining table with a mischievous glint in his eye. And there are so many of us it won't be my turn again for ages and ages and aaaaaaaaaages.

How good that we can resolve things so neatly as a family.

Your daughter,
Eveline

(7)

Oakbeam House
December 18th, 1860

Dear Mother,

I hope you are well in preparations for the festive season; I have gotten a new jelly-mould in the shape of Oakbeam House, you would laugh to see it – it was Matthew's early gift to me but he couldn't wait so now we can use it on the day. I'm going to ask Crabbe to pick up some elderflowers for it – the tree looks glorious all candle-lit and powdered with pretend snow, and ivy and holly weave merrily around the bannisters.

Further correspondence shall come your way directly regarding our arrangements for celebrating as a family; for now, I am simply writing a quick note as I imagine you may have been wondering about how it went with Benson.

He is fine; things went very smoothly and he is in good spirits. I would be lying if I said there were no tears on the day: for the other children began to tease him and play-tend he was about to undergo something very horrible, and this got him frightened. Or perhaps he would have worried himself anyway for, with the best of intentions, Matthew and I cannot help but purse our lips a little when we think of it, and maybe he picked up on our own dread and it became his own. But it was all well, in the end. Matthew took him in the carriage and apparently the Landlord was as lovely as ever and the surgeon gave him a stick of sugar-rock afterwards. Benson is still walking with a bit of a sway; he says it has affected his balance more than he was expecting: but he insists that he is already getting used to it. He is as happy as ever.

I am about to take him over to the Fortunes' to play, in fact, for their youngest had their toe done a year ago for their latest round of rent and has been able to advise. (Dare I anticipate a deep bond of friendship between them?)

Merry Beginnings of the festive season, then!
I will write again soon about the Goose.
Your E

(8)

Oakbeam House
Greenwood
March 1st, 1868

Mother—

What do you mean by your previous letter, it being a matter of personal taste? I can imagine you looking askance at the pattern but I don't agree at all that we have chosen the wrong wall-paper for the drawing-room. The design is very apt for our location: all those delicate sprays of violets! Perhaps it would be too much for your parlour as you live in the town, where everything is shrouded up by the endless chimney-smoke and the image of synthetic fauna would only emphasise your distance from the real thing. But, here in Greenwood, it is just right.

The Fortunes have a similar design in their ballroom, in fact. (Although I think it is a bit much, for a ballroom.)

So, apart from being very happy with the new look of the drawing-room, I am reminded that we are once again coming up to rent due. I feel optimistic and calm, much more so than on the previous occasions; indeed as a family we are approaching it with considerable stoicism. I feel it is time take my turn – Sheila has spoken very passionately of wanting it to be her, but only in youthful tantrums, so it is still too soon for that, I think. I have been imagining whether a finger or toe feels best for me. Our thoughts were turned to the subject early because the Landlord has written a polite note to advise us that he will be writing again within the week, upon a matter of minor business. It is odd perhaps, to write us a letter about a letter, but that is his way, very considerate. I'm only mentioning it to you at all because I can hear Crabbe outside readying the horses for Matthew, as he intends to go upon an errand which reminded me of town which reminded me of the post office which reminded me of how the Landlord's second letter should arrive before too long. In fact, I shall race to catch Matthew and give him this letter too for the post—

Yours in all love,
Eveline

(9)

Oakbeam House
March 5th, 1868

Mother—

My hand shakes as I write this.

101

Oh, horror and horror! Thrice horror—

We have received the letter from the Landlord as promised and the only solace is Matthew and I read it privately together in the drawing-room with the children all playing outside or in their rooms and so they did not bear witness to our reaction—

I can hardly write it, Mother—

The rent has gone up. You cannot imagine what to, the newest asking price... I scarcely know how to comprehend it. I don't think I can write it in actual words—

Indeed, my first thought was that it might be a joke, some bleak jest on part of the Landlord, but the look on Matthew's face assured me what I knew already in my heart was true, that it was real – is real – and that it behoves us now to respond.

My hand shakes every time I recall it anew—

Oh God—

Truly I do not know how to proceed. And to think that I had been, not looking forward to it exactly, rent day has hardly been a celebratory affair of course before now, but at least I had relaxed into a general sense of what to expect. And now we are so overthrown, I do not know—

It is so awful, mother! All very well a finger or toe every eight years, but how can we commit to such a barbarity as this... ! What does it mean?

My tears are smudging the ink, I will write again when we have calmed ourselves enough to discuss our options, although fate seems entirely monstrous at the present moment, God help us—

I remain
Your
Eveline

(10)

Oakbeam House
March 21st, 1868

Dear Mother,

Things are a little calmer, I am glad to report. They have had to be, so we do not throw our lives entirely off balance while we deal with the current situation. As overwhelming as it is, there are other things we also need to deal with; Crabbe has requested leave to get married so we have the bother of advertising for a new groundskeeper, &c...

Of course, Matthew and I have been up late every night, deep in discussion; the children are asking why we are always so red-rimmed about the eyes and sunken of countenance. We are currently playing it off as the news of a long-remembered acquaintance passing away and our both being numb with the shock of it, but I hardly expect this to satisfy them for much longer, the eldest are already narrowing their eyes at us. Benson in particular suspects, I believe.

We have been writing to the Landlord daily in protest against this abominable raising of the rent, detailing how devastating it would be for us.

A head, Mother! In what world could we possibly agree? Such a thing would make us killers or suicides—a head is too much, it takes life with it, everyone knows that, it is not 'only' a head, no matter what the Landlord says. He keeps saying he is not asking for anyone's life.

For, yes, he is replying – we have him on the debating platform, at least. Although he is currently unmoving, expressing only regret at the new rent.

We are trying to negotiate him down to an arm. He rejected that initially; so, next, we offered one arm each from both of us, from below the elbow. If he says yes to that, we will argue that one whole arm is much the same as two from below the elbow, as well as being a much better outcome for us as tenants. I am dashing this letter off to you while we wait for his response.

Throughout all this I take solace in the fact Matthew and I are still best friends and a close team. It is good to know we do not have to immediately capitulate but can, and are, able to respond with reasonableness.

Yours in optimism—
Eveline

(11)

Oakbeam House
March 24th 1868
(Afternoon post.)

Dear Mother,

Forgive the scrawl of my script, but once more I find my hand shakes and I am taken all over with nervous agitation that is affecting my handwriting. This is because I do not know what is happening as I write, or what will happen in the immediate future. I am writing to distract myself from how much I do not know: I cannot reconcile myself to any outcome; I have no idea what life will be like for our family by the time night falls. All this is because Matthew has gone off.

Our letters added up to nothing. Things have been immovable on the recent rent increase. The claim is that it is a regrettable rise but a necessary one. And with the due date looming closer, Matthew and I struck upon the idea that Mr Booth may be more agreeable if spoken to in person.

Matthew said he would go since he has seen him before so there is some pre-existing rapport. We agreed whoever of us went, they should go alone, for if we were both to go it might spook the children. It was horrible, so horrible to bid goodbye to him and I have been in a state of unbreathing, shaking, nervous worry ever since. We went over all the possibilities for how the conversation may go and things Matthew will say if the Landlord says this, or argues that, or suggests the other. We've thought of everything, I think. And I believe our case is strong. Although the rent is not due for a month yet, one of the options Matthew and I decided upon – if we can get him to agree to an arm &c – will be to perform the operation while Matthew is there, so the Landlord cannot change his mind afterwards. (Hence it being another strength that we are not both there, so we are not pressured into accepting any kind of arrangement requiring both of us.) So, I know Matthew will be returning but in what state and with what news I do not—

I see the carriage!

Yr
E

(12)

Oakbeam House
March 24th, 1868
(Evening post.)

Mother—

All is lost. Matthew returned from the meeting fully intact

and – worse – having made no progress with our situation. The Landlord was genuinely regretful, Matthew said, which is the only consolation, meagre as it is. He likes us, Matthew said, very much. But: "his hands are tied" he apparently intoned repeatedly, and the upshot is, the rent is what the rent is. Matthew could not even secure a delay on the date that it is due.

I shall write again soon. Having written this much out to you, I have gained a little more confidence, enough to put my mind to the horrible truth of it; and hopefully I can gather together inside myself just enough fortitude that I can bear to tell the children, which is what I must do next, and perhaps we can make the next decisions as a family—

Your daughter,
Eveline

(13)

Oakbeam House
April 3rd, 1868

Mother; please yet again forgive my scrawl for I cannot see the paper I am sitting in the darkness of our bedroom and I do not wish to light the lamp for Matthew has only just gotten to sleep and it is hard enough for him to sleep at the moment so I cannot disturb him, but I need to write to stop myself from screaming – I write this after the latest in a series of long conversations we have been having as a family and I simply cry to think of the situation we are in. The children are being kind which is the worst of all. I shrink back from the horror of it, but will try to write it here and now in the darkness to purge it from my thoughts, so, let me write of how we gathered them all together in the drawing-room and informed them we had news regarding the newest requirements for the payment of the rent and Benson nodded and said he knew it, he was not surprised and we said it is not what you think and he looked frightened then, and let me tell you mother I have never seen Matthew look so haggard as he did in that moment. We informed the children of the situation and the eldest looked aghast and the youngest giggled until the older children explained to them what it meant and once they realised they were inconsolable. Sheila offered to take the very youngest ones and put them to bed and when she came back she said, I have something I would like to say, mother, and she looked so serious and darling that I knew what she was going to say, and I said, I do not ask anything of you sweetheart, and she said, she did not mind, and to please listen to what she had to say first, and she said it is for the good of the rest of the family to be able to live here another eight years and hasn't it been lovely living here so far, she has nothing to complain about and so wouldn't mind, bless the kindness of her soul, and she said, mama why don't you write to Mr Booth and say I am happy for it to be both my legs, which might surely be a fair substitute for a head, and the other children can take it in turns to push me in a chair with wheels, or I could get special crutches, in fact there are all manner of items to make it okay, and I pulled her towards me while she was assuring me she would get used to it in time and I gathered her in my arms and cried because I cannot ask her to make that sacrifice and even if I did we already know such a rent would not be accepted, how is she to know Matthew and I have already offered similar—

It makes no sense, what the Landlord wants, and if those are his terms how long does he think any tenancy will last – he is pricing himself out.

I haven't informed Matthew yet of what Sheila offered because it would surely break him to hear the children being so kind and wishing to aid in the wellbeing of the whole family in such a way, I can only bear to write it to you, mother, because I hope it is clear I would make the same offer for you—

E

(14)

Oakbeam House
April 13th, 1868

Mother,

I am writing this in a state of new calm. It is as though I have gone through a dark storm of despair and come out the other side, and now everything is understandable; for the wind has swept away what doesn't matter, leaving only shining clarity.

The carriage is waiting for me outside. I am all prepared. I have fortified myself with the brandy we were saving for Matthew's birthday. (Apart from anything else, it is an apt drink for rent day.)

I have considered many options and believe I have settled on something that will be, if not definitive, at least useful.

The only thing remaining is to finish this letter so you and Father know what has happened if I do not write again. I have also written a note to Matthew and a longer letter for the children to discover upon waking. Perhaps I will return to them in this world, but I do not know if I shall, nor, at this moment, if I should hope to.

I am aware I have been complicit in our family's terrible situation by being so keen for us to live here and what I wish, need to do is make amends. This, I believe, is how I might do it.

I do not know if the family will be allowed to stay afterwards:

if what I intend to do will be enough. All I know is this: I will not give the rent that is being asked. None of us will pay that appalling price. I am reconciled to sacrificing myself but I would die with my head attached, and secure a moral victory. I am frightened; my hand shakes, I blot the ink. No matter. The wind is coming through the window casements; I might also take this opportunity to note the paint is coming chipped in the pantry these days and all the once-shining brass is tarnished on the fixtures; perhaps some of the workmanship on this house is shoddier than we first understood it to be.

Your loving daughter—
Always.
Eveline

P.S. Please inform any friends or acquaintances of yours who may express an interest that Greenwood remains, in my estimation, a decent place to live overall, although the rent is newly steep.

THE ROT
LAUREN ARCHER

I – SPORE

The rot sits, with grim certainty, at the corner of my bedroom window. There, it has eaten away at the wood, causing the magnolia paint to peel back in thin spools, pigment puckered like flesh under flame. The timber beneath is riddled with deep cracks, ruptured and flaking away, exposing a dark, sodden core. I reach out to touch it and a large splinter comes away in my hand. The shard lies in the creases of my cupped palm, roughly the size and shape of a canine tooth, wet and unnaturally heavy. Its fibrous point is caked in a chalky red residue, as though freshly plucked from a bleeding gum.

I set the splinter down on my desk, the last in a row of all the chunks of rotten wood I have collected since moving in here three months ago. Mounting evidence of the rot's impact; proof that I am not imagining its slow encroach.

The carcass of last night's drawing lies in the centre of the desk, the paper soft and furry with lines drawn, erased and redrawn. The helix of a spiral staircase rendered in mechanical pencil winds around itself on the page, a perfect nautiliform swirl with an ornate handrail coils around the perimeter of the curve.

As I look at it a moment longer, the lines begin to falter, running into each other at odd angles. The scale looks off. Each step collides into the one after it with brute force. I imagine the staircase collapsing in on itself, sending its user hurtling down into the blank space below. I tear the perforated page off and fold the sheet once, twice, as many times as possible until the drawing disappears into the folds. It falls into the bin beneath the desk, where it joins a long history of other discarded drawings.

Although the area around the desk is clear of rot, its presence lurks behind me. When I turn around, I expect to find it changed somehow: spreading across the window, clouding the glass and tarnishing the frosted panes with powdery spores. But, of course, it remains the same. It intrudes slowly, centimetre by centimetre, when I leave it unattended. A small expansion while I am on the bus to work, another while I am sat eating lunch at my desk. If I go away for a weekend to stay with my parents, I can measure its development in centimetres with my scale ruler on my return.

I try to remember how many times I have called the property management company.

The first was days after I first moved in. I tried to open the window one afternoon and let the last dregs of September sun into my room, and a small chunk of the sill yielded and gave way in my hands. Since that first cleaving, it has worsened steadily. It waits until I am out of the house and creeps further across the windowsill, repelling paintwork and splintering the wood as it goes. I have not opened the window since that last September day, but the spores drift through the room regardless, as though propelled by a breeze. There we sit, the rot and me, breathing the same air.

I don't know how I missed it in the viewing. I spent long, hot days going from flat to flat, accompanied by an interchangeable cast of estate agents. I wasn't in a position to turn anything liveable down. I have never, really, been in the position to turn anything liveable down. I sent endless enquiries and viewed everything I could, using up most of my holiday allowance to take day trips around my own city and look around small flats full of flat pack furniture and black pleather sofas, papery spherical IKEA lampshades and 2-in-1 fridge freezers. Shared kitchens with assigned food cupboards and shared bathrooms with a crowd of different brightly coloured bottles of body wash and shampoo.

I filled in forms stipulating my small salary and naming my parents as a guarantor, despite knowing I would never actually ask them for help. I received a lot of sorries and unfortunatlies, a lot of requests for admin fees that I thought had been outlawed and vague references to deposit holding schemes. Eventually, I got a place — this place — and moved my things in a single trip from the flat I used to share with Emily. Now, when I roll over in bed in search of her warmth, all I find instead is the rot.

I found the flat on a website for matching up potential housemates. The advert read: 'Small, affordable room in three bed flat. Good transport links to city centre. Some original features. Quiet, tidy house would prefer quiet, tidy housemate.' I have not seen the other residents once since the day I received the keys.

The house, number 23, is a Victorian terrace which has been dissected over the years into ever smaller portions. Gutted and split in half in the post-war years, then flayed into four flats inthe early 90s. This flat, my flat, is on the ground floor, wedged between the young family in the one above and a group of students in the basement. Between the screams of the two toddlers charging around above our heads and the screams of the pre- and post-drinks beneath us, there is rarely an extended period of quiet. Often, just as the relief of a party dying downstairs permits me to roll over in bed and hope for sleep, the scraping jingle of early morning children's television will rouse me.

I don't spend much time in the communal rooms. The living room is narrow, like a crawl space between a two-person sofa and a wall-mounted television. I only sit in there on rare occasions, but the forced proximity to the screen always reminds me of that one scene in *A Clockwork Orange* and puts me off whatever I'm watching. At the corridor's far end lies this kitchen, a poorly extended space which juts out beyond the natural boundaries of the house. It never feels quite solid. The walls are all wrong. They are frail and papery, seeming to sway in the breeze that drifts perpetually through. Even on still days, the flat moves. Air leaks in around closed windows and under locked doors, whistling through the house, rustling the leaves of my wilting monstera plant and sending the stack of old bills by the front door up in a flurry.

When I leave my room, the kitchen door is wedged slightly ajar at the end of the narrow corridor. Behind it, there is the soft clatter and splash of someone washing up. The tap gushes into the sink; cutlery clatters against crockery. I return to my room to get my lanyard for work and by the time I am back in the corridor again, the kitchen is silent, the door firmly shut. When I open it, I find the room dark and empty. A thin layer of dust sits on the dirty dishes in the sink.

I cook porridge on the hob, sparking the gas with a lighter because the ignition doesn't work. Flames lick the bottom of the pan. I fill a mug with water and another with oats and stir them together with a pinch of salt, turning the mixture over and over until it comes together in a gelatinous heap. Eating straight from the pan, I dig a teaspoon into the steaming mound and take quick, successive bites, trying to warm myself in the cold, damp air of the kitchen.

I have lived in many such unhomely homes. From my university halls, where I slept up against a wall peppered with Blu Tack stains – the ghosts of someone else's personalisation – to the eight-bedroom shrine to decaying grandeur I shared with a loose group of friends for the first few months after graduation.

The only time I ever really felt at home was with Emily. Our flat was not much better than this one: cramped, damp, cheaply partitioned. And yet, with her, all those shortcomings were immaterial. She framed posters from gigs we'd been to together and hung them over the bleak magnolia walls. She covered every surface with candles and incense sticks, so that the smell of damp was undercut by vanilla, lavender and sandalwood. When, one day, she told me she wanted me to move out, I realised that none of the pretty things that had made our home were mine. She said that was part of the problem.

I have never known how to make a place comfortable. I studied architecture at university; I have loved buildings my whole life but cannot ever reconcile with the idea that perhaps they do not love me back.

While I am eating, I catch sight of the corner of the kitchen, where the white wall meets the skirting board. There, the familiar pucker of paint announces the rot's presence. Uninvited, it has joined me for breakfast. I linger, staring at it, for too long and do not notice the rising steam until a sharp sensation pricks my hand. I draw it back to reveal a row of white blisters dotted across the soft skin that runs from my little finger to my wrist. I drop the teaspoon and hold my hand under the cold tap, wincing as the water runs over the shiny surface of my new skin. Returning to the pan, I put the lid on and the trapped steam rises up against the lid. From the kitchen drawer, I take a pack of post-its and a pen and leave one stuck to the pan which reads: 'feel free to eat leftovers!'

As I turn to leave, I notice the grey laminate tiles of the kitchen are covered in iridescent trails. They glisten in the half-light of morning. They start at the garden door, lead over the tiles and past the fridge, wind around chair and table legs, over the patch beneath my feet and back the way they came. Snails. The benefit of the ground floor is, apparently, the ease of access to the communal garden. But it also grants the garden access to us.

It faces me now as I look out of the kitchen window. Garden is a grand term. It is, rather, a square patch of concrete hemmed in at three sides by fences. The only living thing is a predatory patch of bindweed which has asphyxiated every other plant. At the garden's centre is a white plastic table and three chairs, the fourth lying in a mangled heap in the far corner, one leg snapped off. The chairs and table are covered in a rash of green mould, the centre of the grooves almost black. I sat out there only once, bringing with me a paperback book and a can of cheap lager on that same last hot week in September. I lasted only half an hour or so, until I thought I saw a curtain on the first-floor twitch and felt, at once, the chill of so many cold stares on my soft, pale body. Emily used to tell me how much she liked the way I looked. She would run a finger along the curve of my back, lay her hand to rest on my thigh. Even then, it was hard to translate her words, her touch, into something I believed. Now, without them, my body has once again become something I am uncertain of, a space I occupy that is at once too big and too small to fit properly.

As I lock the front door and set out for the bus stop, I have that same sensation again. Too many pairs of eyes watching as I disappear around the corner. I know, logically, that it is morning and everyone except the screeching toddlers and their soft-eyed mother is likely asleep, but I feel, at once, every resident of the dismembered house watching me: my elusive housemates, the party-hardened students of the basement flat, the snails, the rot.

I sit at the top deck of the bus and watch the suburbs contract and mutate into the skyscrapers and flat blocks of the city centre. The blisters send little shivers of pain up through my arm whenever I mistakenly lay my hands to rest in my lap. I pick at one until it oozes and bleeds, which pools out onto the sleeve of my cardigan. Initially, this sense of reopening provides some comfort, but soon the shock of red against soft lilac wool appals me, and I try to cover my mistake with the other hand. 'Don't *pick* at it', my mother would have said, but she is cities away at her kitchen table and unable to warn me.

The bus groans into my stop and coughs out a puddle of commuters. It's a short walk to the office, an anonymous glass block in the belly of the city. My green lanyard grants me access to the foyer and allows me behind the turnstiles. It also distinguishes me from other members of staff: blue for architects, yellow for management, red for technologists and green for admin. We are, notably, a secondary colour. I pause by the lift doors to relish the last of the sunlight, before stepping inside and pressing the down button, feeling the car shudder and then begin the descent to the basement. When the lift doors open on the fifth floor, I join a sea of green lanyards, each one typing an email or answering a phone, moving information around while those in the floors above us rebuild the city. The job, of course, pays a meagre amount, over half of which I spend on my room and the company of the rot. Ostensibly, this is in exchange for a forty-hour week, but one which often bloats and bulges over into fifty, sixty or more.

"You will have to be prepared to work some evenings and weekends, due to the nature of the industry," a short-fringed woman in horn-rimmed glasses told me at my interview, leaning in and smiling widely as though I was being offered an exciting secret opportunity. Yes, I told her, I am absolutely prepared. I imagined myself gracefully ducking between waiters dispersing canapes and gifted people staring in concentrated silence at white paper models. In reality, most of the 'out of hours' work is administration: answering the phone in the clamouring cold of a 4am in winter to take notes of from a sister company in Shanghai; being warned to never, ever use the out of office setting on my email.

Silence is made impossible in the office, always, by the purr of the photocopier. The noise permeates my concentration, serving as the sole soundtrack to my day. One of the other green lanyards stands at the machine, feeding it documents which it swallows hungrily. With each whir, the open list casts a bright light over him, illuminating his face from below and carving out each crease and crack in shadow.

Both phones ring at once and the secretaries answer in unison, twin voices joined in joyful professionalism.

"You're through to Head Office! Please hold!"

I am copied into an email chain about an exhibition in an art gallery that the firm is sponsoring. An interior photographer based in London. I have been included, assumedly, by mistake. The email chain is hundreds of messages long, each one replied to or forwarded on to an ever-lengthening list of representatives from the associated organisations. Within the sticky web of correspondence is a link to an online portfolio of the photographer's work. Black and white photographs in eye watering high definition, taken at odd angles which serve to isolate their subjects from the contexts they belong in. Billowing curtains flank bay windows; Turkish rugs expand to fill drawing rooms; Chesterfield sofas serve as dog beds for quivering chihuahuas and goblin-faced bulldogs.

The attached copy reads:

'Intimate friend of the Belgravia, Mayfair and Hyde Park elite, Adrian Swift invites viewers to take an indulgent sojourn in some of the nation's most impressive private properties. These images, which teasingly straddle the line between voyeurism and visitation, reveal the intimate intricacies that make up aspirational aesthetics.'

I pin the email so that I can look back at the photos later, and I move on to meetings. With one hand typing on the keyboard and the other holding my foil-wrapped sandwich, I schedule video calls between Swiss landscape architects and a parks department in Toronto, a civil engineer in Southampton and a sculptor in Hong Kong. Every time an invite is sent out, my email refreshed automatically and the number in the little red circle hovering at the periphery of the icon increases. I have 24, then 31, then 38 new emails. The more I try to deplete the pile, the higher the number seems to rise. There is the exuberant ping of new mail, then the whir of the photocopier, then the shrill "You're through to Head Office! Please hold!" always, always in unison and then back to the ping and then it's 6 o'clock and I've accidentally worked too late again and the office is empty and I've missed the bus.

When I return home, the hallway is dark and cold. The house is waiting quietly; patiently. I resolve to have a bath, draw, sleep and call the property management company on the way to work.

II – HYPHAE

I try to make it nice. I light an old Christmas candle, hoping the smell of pine needles will evoke a rural atmosphere. In the absence of a speaker, I lean my phone against the medicine cabinet and play some instrumental music. The sound bounces off the metal and reverberates a tinny approximation of the original song. I step into the bath, the warm water welcoming my goose-bumped legs. Bubbles gather around my body, clutching at exposed skin. I try to close my eyes, but I cannot help but stare at the far edge of the bath, where mildew lurks in the spaces between the tiles and along the seamline of white porcelain.

The rot is always with me. Even when I escape to another corner of the house, or down the street and onto the bus that takes me to work. Wherever I am, it finds me. It is in the black mould that seems to ooze from the edges of the kitchen sink. It is in the thick condensation on the windowpanes and the slick wetness of walls. Even here, in the sanctity of the bath, it takes the form of mildew and gazes at me longingly from behind the taps.

I wash half-heartedly, feeling as though I am simply moving dirt around rather than clearing it. Every time I run the sponge over my right arm, I find it looks grimier than before. I trace the skin with my other hand, feeling a strange and unfamiliar surface beneath my fingers. I am used to my body feeling strange, to prodding at my doughy flesh and picking at my skin, but this is something different.

I pull the plug and the water level falls, drips of soapy liquid filtering down the drain. As I am towelling off, my skin feels weirder still. I examine myself under the harsh white glow of the strip light. White filaments have sprawled across the surface of my arm, reaching up from my hand, winding around my forearm. I brush them off with the towel and they drift down to the bathmat. Although my arm looks bare, I can still feel the patterns they made on my skin. Winding rivulets and estuaries, drifting in and out of each other.

I bend down to examine them, holding the strands up under the light. A spiderweb of small threads, creating a thin, downy mesh. I gather as many as I can and stuff them into the bathroom bin, watching as they disappear with the lid's snap. Even from within the bin, they emanate a dense, musty smell.

When I search the internet for my symptoms, I find a scientifically unsubstantiated illness which is categorised as either dermatological or delusional, depending on who you ask. I am unsure which is worse: a degenerative condition which results in fibrous sores erupting all over my body or a psychiatric issue which means I hallucinate fibrous sores erupting all over my body. The images, when I get to them, are horrifying and my skin starts to itch just from looking at them. Real or imagined, the only thing doctors seem to agree on is that the condition has its roots in skin picking, so I resolve to leave the blisters to heal.

In hopes of taking my mind off this strange new condition, I sit at my desk and draw. An etched plan for an expansive public building that will never exist. A vast canopy, an ornate gilded façade. I am in a mess of pencil shavings and rubber detritus, my hand cramping and the skin on my middle finger leathery with use. Around me, the house sits in a slow, stony silence. No sound at all. Not even the tinny rattle of canned laughter from an American TV series on a laptop or the rustle of a cold body under covers.

Suddenly, a door slam punctuates the quiet and I hear two pairs of feet moving across the laminate floor. A giggle. The soft clatter of keys dropped into the dish and the slam of the fridge door opening and closing. Can I hear the grind of aluminium thread as a wine bottle is opened, the gargle as it is poured into glasses? I know, logically, that the kitchen is too far away to permit that, and yet every sound seems magnified. In the corridor now, the noises get louder and louder; whispers translate into booming shouts, muffled laughter to merciless hysterics. It is as though they are in the room with me, clinking wine glasses together and kicking off shoes. Something possesses me and I rise out of my chair and towards the bedroom door, hoping, perhaps, to intercept them and be brought into their evening. As I stand at the door, I feel them on the other side, can picture the hazy eyes, the mismatched glasses of saccharine corner shop chardonnay. I open the door, prepared to meet them brightly, and find the corridor empty. A chill runs the length of it, the dead air of unused space. I strain to hear the noises but they are gone.

I release the door and let it close, abandoning my drawings and crawling into bed, dragging my laptop in with me like a

reluctant lover. I watch three episodes of a TV show in which
the presenter tours around small and unusual living spaces:
treehouses, garden sheds, an old circus wagon. In each episode,
he marvels at the ingenuity of the homemakers who, with
an assumedly vast injection of money, have turned their tiny
residences into architectural feats worthy of a Channel 4 film
crew. I fall asleep with the show still playing, the whimsical
jaunt of the theme tune leaking into my dreams.

My sleep is rough and restless. I wake at seemingly endless
intervals. My subconscious takes me up in glass elevators and
down into subterraneous bunkers, through grand banqueting
halls and across courtyards laced with lilac wisteria and plump
yellow roses. I dream that I am travelling in a relentless loop in
the compartment of a paternoster lift, unable to step off onto
my platform. I wake to the sensation of falling.

In another pocket of sleep, I am ducking through a cavernous
cellar, dust falling from above me and blanketing the hard floor.
Without warning, the dust turns a rusty red. I wake up gasping,
the brassy residue coating my arms, my chest, my face. I blink
back red tears and then, when I open my eyes, the room is dark
once more and I cannot bring myself to turn on the light.

I wake suddenly, moments before my alarm. My phone lies
on my bedside table and I reach over to silence it before the
alert can interrupt the quiet of the morning. I turn on the lamp,
expecting a layer of russet dust to be sitting on top of my duvet,
but I can see nothing but the off-white of over-washed cotton. As
I pull the covers back, the shallow beam illuminates tendrils of
white floss that have reformed on my hand and arm overnight.
I hold my foreign limb up curiously. Turning it left and right, I
examine the prying strands. They look wet, almost sticky, but
when I reach out with my free hand, they feel soft and furry.

Again, I peel them off and discard them, leaving them on
my bedside table, balled up like string. When I examine my skin

once again in the bathroom, it looks fine. I can see no obvious source of infection. Even the blisters on my hand has begun to heal, the dry, perforated edge toughening and cleaving back to the surrounding skin. I am in no pain or discomfort, not even a mild itch as proof that the alien body was ever there.

I get out of bed and go over to the window where the rot has spread further still. Wetness reaches out from the woodwork to the wall and spots of mould have begun to form. A postcard I had tacked up there, from a childhood trip to Southwell Minster, has fallen. It lies, face down, on the grey carpet. When I reach to retrieve it, the paper is damp to the touch and the glossy coating has started to peel at the edges. The rot looks at me and I look back. The magnolia paint bubbles and blisters. The spores dance in the early morning sun and settle as a fine layer of orange dust across the carpet. I feel a heady compulsion to be elsewhere.

The kitchen table is littered with the remnants of somebody else's party. Crushed beer cans and empty bottles of wine stand at the centre, accompanied by a flurry of stray tobacco, cigarette ends and ash. One of my bowls has been repurposed as an ashtray, the sodden mess of spilt beer and wet rizla forming a grim deposit at the bottom. The mass of debris seems impossible, given that I only heard two voices last night. Two voices and then nothing at all.

On the hob, my pot of porridge is sat festering. I remove the lid and find a claggy mass, ignored by my housemates and forgotten by me. I try to scrape it into the bin, and it comes out in a single heap which hits the bottom of the bin with a dull thud. As I move towards the sink to wash up, I feel a cold sensation beneath my socked foot. Something that is both sharp and soft. I lift my foot up and watch as a stringy, gelatinous mass of sinew and shell comes with it. The ooze is speckled with fragmented pieces of the snail's crushed exterior, like shards of eggshell whisked into yolk. I decide to abandon breakfast.

The hold music for the property management company is a haunting run through of the top hits from a period long enough ago that they are no longer relevant but not long enough ago that they have acquired a nostalgic pleasantry. I wait on hold for twenty-seven minutes.

"I'm calling about the rot," I say, once somebody answers the phone.

The man on the other end asks where I live but doesn't ask my name.

"Flat two."

He asks which flat two.

"Cavendish Road."

He asks which of their houses on Cavendish Road.

"23."

He sighs as though I have already done something wrong although I cannot imagine what. Then he asks if he can put me on hold. Before I can speak, he hangs up and leaves me listening to a male vocalist jump through several wavering key changes over a synthy melody. When we are reconnected, he explains with painstaking slowness and care as though I am very stupid and very small, that a structural survey will be carried out on the property as soon as possible. He also advises me against using the word rot until the surveyor clarifies that this is, in fact, what we are dealing with.

"Ok. Well, what would you like me to call it then?"

He pauses for an exceptionally long time before suggesting we refer to it as 'the affected area.'

"Right. The thing is, I rang you about the *affected area* when I first moved in, three months ago, which is when you said you would arrange for a structural survey as soon as possible. So, I'm just calling back to try to work out when the structural survey is actually going to happen so we can get the rot – the *affected area* – sorted out. I can't keep paying my rent to live in a rotting – *affected* – flat."

At the mention of the rent, the unnamed man on the other side of the phone conducts a sharp inhale. I can practically hear the synapses firing in his brain, the mental calculations clacking like an abacus. He wraps the call up quickly and I am left alone, the bus rattling through streets of identical terraced houses with identical front gardens of gravel and paving slab and astroturf. The sky is the inky blue of winter morning, fading to yellow at the horizon like a day-old bruise.

III – MYCELIUM

Down in the basement, the day gets away from me bit by bit and then all at once. I arrive at work without any solid memory of the journey there. I send another email to the property management company, which bounces back immediately citing a non-existent destination. I call from my desk phone and arrive at the voicemail for a pizza restaurant in Shrewsbury; I call again and someone with a thick Glaswegian accent answers and tells me to leave them alone. On my third attempt, I am told that calls to this number are barred and by my sixth I realise hours have drifted by, it is already lunchtime and the desk phone isn't plugged in.

I spend my lunch break in the bathroom stall, husking my cardigan and looking at the reformed growth on my arm. It has travelled further still. It winds up and over my shoulder blade, across my clavicle, reaching out to my left side. Little offshoots pulse in the space between my chest and face, threatening to meander up my neck and over the line of my jaw. When I check my phone, I realise there are only two minutes left of my lunch break. I feel a familiar panic rise inside me. It feels wrong, somehow, to deposit the filamentous heap in the work toilets and so, before I can consider it any further, I have buttoned up my cardigan and carried on with my day.

After lunch, I take notes in a meeting about a new luxury lifestyle complex planned by an oversees developer. In the promotional pamphlet, attractive people roughly my age run on treadmills in the gym and swim lengths in the heated indoor pool. I write for the entire time, making notes of site boundaries and building regulations to be typed up later. I write until the leathery patch of skin on the inside of my middle finger is smooth and blackened with biro ink. I try to focus on the details of the build, to subdue thoughts of the rot which linger in my mind, but at the end of the meeting when I flick back through my notebook, I don't recognise any of the words I have written. Lines of confused correspondence collapse into margins. Characters alternate wildly between lower case and capital; some letters appear back to front and inside out.

When I look down, I see the braids of white emerging from beneath my cardigan sleeve and wrapping around my wrist, like the strangulating stems of bindweed. I pull my sleeve down hurriedly, hoping to hide it from the panel of primary colour lanyards that surround me. When I look around the room, I see that everyone is staring down at their tablets. Nobody is looking at me. In fact, I realise, nobody has looked at me for quite some time.

I spend the last hour of my working day – and quite some time beyond that – looking through the photographs again. A dark carpet runs down the spine of a wide, marbled staircase. A fireplace is gutted out and stuffed with amputated logs. A pair of porcelain Staffordshire spaniels stare directly at the camera with lifeless eyes. There is a whole series of front doors: thick, heavy, with brass knockers. In one, the knocker is in the shape of a cat's writhing tail. In another, it takes the form of a ring clasped between a wolf's jaw. I click and click through the photos, going all the way through them and then back to the start. When I move my hand to the keyboard to type an email, something pulls me back. A single white stalk, like the petiole of a leaf, is running along my index finger and connecting me to the computer mouse. I wrench my hand back in instinct and the stalk snaps, leaving a soft white residue on the mouse's black plastic surface.

As the evening gives way into the liminal space between one day and another, there are noises in the hallway once more. The low, slow creak of the front door opening. The soft clatter of a pair of high heels dropped on the welcome mat. Stifled laughter, a cough. A guttural growl. The kitchen door opens and then slams frankly. From behind two shut doors, I can make out the drone of music and the hush of lowered voices. I wonder, briefly, what state the kitchen will be in when I get up for work tomorrow morning. I do not step into the hallway. Instead, I keep drawing.

A new sound begins and grows steadily in volume. For a moment, it sounds like it is coming from the rot; from the dank corner where the tainted wood is giving way. It builds to a low moan. I want to jump up and tear the rotting wood out with my hands, to scoop it out in chunks and throw it to the carpeted floor. Then, the noise again. From the far corner of the room this time. A frenzied rustle, like something clamouring within the walls, inside the empty chamber between my room and the next. It dies down for a moment, then returns, joined by a metallic creak and a banshee wail. The shock of the sudden change of pitch forces my hand across the paper, rupturing its surface. The noises – the rustle, the creak, the wail – unite and become rhythmic. A pulse. It is then that I realise that the noises are not creatures living in the walls, or the slow, solemn force of the rot. They are the animal noises of one of my housemates finding a warm body with which to share the night.

I plug in my headphones and return to my drawing. Beyond the window, beyond the rot, the outer recesses of the city begin to fall asleep. One light turns off, then another. A fox meanders through the spilled orange light of street lamp. A car alarm starts and stops. The glow of my laptop casts a harsh shadow across the desk and, for tonight, the rot is hidden in the dark recess. But I know it is there. I draw late into the night and early into the morning. My hand feels tight, my fingers cramping with use. Scattered around me are a selection of stubby pencils, a compass, a scale ruler. My hand is cast in greyscale – the gunmetal of graphite shavings against the bright white of the growth.

In my dreams, Romanesque arches dwarf me on all sides, layers of brick rising up to hem me in. A crown spire pierces me through the middle, the four regal points of the steeple pinning my four limbs to flying buttresses. I tumble over a parapet. I land on the waiting spikes of wrought iron railings. Walled up in a catacomb, my body is scattered with fragments of stained glass, glorious sunlight spilling over my technicolour corpse.

IV – FRUITING BODY

The harsh light of my desk lamp filters through my eyelids, filling my head with a soft red glow. I realise, with a start, that I have fallen asleep at my desk. Drawings pile up on my desk. Huge, sprawling designs on A3 bond paper taped down at all corners. Hurried sketches on torn scraps of notebook. A miniature the size of a stamp on the back of a receipt.

Each one is a monstrous creation.

The buildings I have designed are ragged and lopsided. The roofs collapse amid imbalanced beams; the staircases turn in and in on themselves, leading nowhere. One has only interior windows. Another has too many walls and not enough corners.

An ache builds in my hand and travels up my wrist, creeping up from the intersection of my forefinger and thumb to the crook of my elbow. I am still holding my pen. It has been nestled in my hand for eight hours or more, leaving a dark mark at its tip that bulges out across the page. I try to tear my hand away, but I am pinned down, thick white strands tying me to the desk's surface. A throbbing mass, spreading in all directions like the branches of a tree or the roots of a plant.

The skin of my right arm is no longer visible beneath the writhing network of writhing network of capillaries. At intersections, the white threads converge and weave in and out of each other, knotting together and forming thick, fibroid mounds. They continue to expand, pulsating as they grow. Each stem sends another out from it, like bronchioles in search of fresh air.

At the crease of my wrist, where the most mature strands of matter lie, small mushrooms sprout, with deep orange centres and wide frilly caps in brilliant white. They expand and multiply, bursting up towards the lamp's glow. Soon, my arm is spined with a long row of mushrooms. A wet, earthy smell like turned soil fills the air. The room is thick with their rust-coloured spores. They settle on the floor as a thick carpet of dust and fill the deep crevasses of the creased duvet.

The webs widen, tracking across my body, down my torso and towards my legs. Some reach out for my left side, not content with absorbing just a single limb. Others are at my throat, undulating, fanning out and wrapping themselves around my neck.

The downy tip of a single tendril reaches my lower lip. Beyond my room, there is a soft rumbling like somebody boiling the kettle, but I cannot be sure that it is not the low gurgle of the bubbling paintwork, or the groan of the mushrooms fruiting on my shoulder. I cannot be sure that there is even anybody else in

the flat. Either way, I realise, I do not know my housemates well
enough to scream for help.

THE CITY WHERE ONE FINDS THE LOST
LERAH MAE BARCENILLA

Every night, I have the same dream.

It always starts at the House.

The floorboards are rotten, the walls weep. But it is only when the makahiya leaves claw through the wood that I realise I am dreaming. This time, I am on the second floor, in the entresuelo where I can peer down at the ground floor, over the edge of the antesala's wooden barriers. A lone piano stands on one side of the long corridor that stretches before me, leading to the sala mayor and beyond, to the bedrooms. With every step, the wood squelches beneath my shoes, damp with rot and soil.

I know I am dreaming and yet—

The makahiya leaves tremble as I near. Curl into themselves as I walk by. Empty shelves line the corridor walls and the books that once filled them are scattered across the floor with their pages ripped apart, yellowing paper eaten by moths. The porcelain vases hold dried stems. Moths with mottled wings that look like eyes flutter above the heads of dried dahlias. Their fragile petals crumble to ash, scattering in the quiet breeze which has slipped through the stained lace curtains.

Beyond the open Capiz windows, rice fields stretch as far as I can see beneath distant flickering stars. I swallow against the heavy, sour air, a lingering scent of stale wood polish, mothballs and the sharp scent of dying flowers.

I know I am no longer alone.

There is someone at the end of the corridor.

The girl is wearing a traje de mestiza; a white lace camisa with delicate bell-shaped sleeves and a flared, embroidered skirt. Her long, black hair falls in wavy tresses over her shoulders pulled together with a delicate, blue bow. Under the darkness, she is an ivory butterfly. And though the shadow hides her face, I know I won't forget the curl of that red, red smile.

There is a mirror hanging on the wall behind her, framed with gold and flowers. She steps out of view with a swish of her dress, a ghost in the periphery and when I blink, she appears at the bottom of the staircase.

Anastacia looks up at me with those golden eyes.

She disappears through the double doors without glancing back.

The metal gates leading to the garden are open, and even from a glance, I know the flowers are long dead. Even the fruit trees are not spared. They stand with empty branches, a pile of dried leaves at their roots. Not far away are their rotten fruits, piling in small, festering mounds, plagued by the buzzing flies picking at their over-ripe skins.

There is a flicker of white in my periphery and I follow, stepping into the streets of Sangbulawan. It is not the Sangbulawan I know.

The church that stands at the heart of the town has fallen. Its tower has been severed in half and the pillars that once held it together are but piles of debris on the dry ground. Large, rotten roots wrap around the fallen stone like serpents and orchids bloom where the cracks have appeared. The barangay hall is missing its eastern side, as though a large claw had swiped it into rumble. The globe in the plaza is cracked in half and the statue of a rider atop a horse, some general long lost to time, is missing his head. Santan flowers used to grow here in rows. All that remains are wilted, blackened petals, with moths fluttering on the dead leaves like wraiths. The marketplace lies abandoned, wooden tables upturned and split in half, fabrics torn with something thin and sharp.

With every step I take, the earth crumbles beneath my feet. Makahiya leaves tear through the cracks, followed by vines of orchids with spotted petals. They wrap around my ankles rooting me in place, carving thin red lines across my legs like tallies.

All I can do is watch.

Anastacia stands at its centre, at the crossroads between the fallen church and the derelict marketplace.

Her back is always towards me when she whispers, "Isn't it beautiful?" with a tilt of her head and I hear her voice as though she is right beside me.

From her mouth emerge what appears to be a million white butterflies, a surge of wings that clog my throat, catching words on my tongue, choking against the sour-sweet air——

Then, I wake, gasping, as though I had spent hours underwater and only now found air.

"Did you have a bad dream?" The swish of fabric and light streams into the room in hazy lines. Anastacia comes into view, face stained with sunlight. She leans closer and pokes me on the forehead with a delicate finger. "Is it the same one?"

"Yes." My voice sounds hoarse even to my ears. I blink away the sleep in my eyes. "Always the same one." Unlike the Anastacia in my dreams, this one wears a white dress made of piña. Her collarbones are framed with an elaborate embroidery of flowers, dahlias and vines orchids, among others I cannot name. The bell-shaped sleeves remain – still a butterfly even in the waking world. I reach over to trace a finger against her sleeve in thought. I can feel those eyes studying me. "What's the occasion?"

"It's Sunday," she tuts, curling a hand around my wrist and pulling me out of the blankets. "We'll be late."

There is a story my Lola used to tell us when we were little.

It is a story about loss and about an invisible city.

Tumao. Araw. Biringan.

"Hanapan ng mga nawawala."

The city 'where one finds the lost'.

Its name changes depending on who you ask and where.

Perhaps there are many similar cities.

Or there is only one.

They say that this city boasts towering spires, ancient cathedrals and architecture one would see only beyond the archipelago. The city of never-ending twilight.

They say this city holds anything one could ever desire.

Some people in the barangay even whisper that there is one in the forest surrounding our little town. And the reason that the elders always warn us away from wandering too far is because of its inhabitants.

They say it is the home of engkantos.

Or the souls of the lost and the dead.

The story changes every time depending on who you ask.

I like to think it is the latter. That the city is a form of heaven where you can reunite with your beloved, where time is inconsequential, where death is null.

In some stories it is prison, in others, paradise.

But one thing always remains consistent —you must never eat food given by its inhabitants.

Wriggling black rice.

The sweetest of fruits.

If you eat them, even just one bite, you are trapped.

There are many stories in our barangay of those who have been enticed by strangers from the forest. Many sightings of a beautiful girl with a crown of thorns carved with dripping gold that slide down her cheeks like tears. The ridge between her sharp nose and rambutan-red lips is missing.

She appears either familiar, or from out of town.

They say that, if you catch their eyes, they will do anything in their power to bring you back to their city. They will persuade you to eat their food and you will be lost to the land of the living. There is no saving those who are taken by the city.

I often wondered what the city would look like. I thought that the best way to entice someone to stay within its walls was for the city to take the shape of a place that feels like home.

Would it appear as your childhood house? Flood-worn shelves lined with old, ragged toys and books filled with stories you heard as a child, and your grandmother waiting for you in the living room.

Would it appear as a replica of the city you spent your favourite summers in? Down to the small bakery your mother often brought you to that makes your favourite pandesal, with just the right softness at the centre?

I often wondered – in the curious way a child wondered – what the city would look like to me.

Every Sunday there is mass. Every Sunday, we open our gates and follow a procession of familiar faces along the one, paved road leading into the heart of the barangay.

The church towers over all the other buildings. Inside, someone has put up bamboo rafters to work on the roofs. The priest's sermon, combined with the heat and the smell of incense, has made my thoughts foggy. I watch as a flock of maya birds play hide and seek, their mottled wings disappearing in between the hollow wood.

Anastacia nudges me in the rib. Her golden bracelets jingle as she waves an embroidered fan under her chin, the wafts of air sending strands of hair fluttering over her shoulders. When she notices my gaze, she leans closer until I can feel the cool air against my skin. I fidget in my piña dress, wipe at my forehead with one of Anastacia's handkerchiefs. A few weeks ago, I sat with her in the garden as she sewed a red dahlia at the centre of the fabric with careful, delicate fingers. When I catch her eyes, she flicks her chin towards the altar. For the rest of the sermon, my mind does not stray.

The forest that surrounds our barangay stretches for miles on all sides, only broken by one lonely road that leads to the nearest city. It is an ancient beast with many different towering trees that cover the sky and stars and flowers that would make even Madame de la Luna's garden look tame in comparison.

It is easy to get lost in there.

And once, I did.

I can't remember precisely, but I remember stepping over the boundary of our town, from paved paths to overgrown moss and damp soil, past the trees, into the heart of the forest. It swallows you up, the overgrowth, and I remember the dizzying, disorienting feeling of trees surrounding me. I had no sight of any building, their branches stirring, leaves rustling like distant voices. I remember my grandmother's stories. Of how the forest can deceive. Of what lives in the trees. I remember the taste of fear at the tip of my tongue, sweet like overripe fruit.

I thought I was lost forever.

That was the first time I met Anastacia.

I've never found out who led me out of that forest, but I remember waking up in my bed with sweat clinging to my brows, the fabric of my blankets plastered against my body and my skin laid over my bones like an unfamiliar weight. I had a fever. The forest felt like a bad dream.

I was eleven. My Lola was worried, perhaps, that I had been lured into the trees, that something still clung to me even as I escaped. She had sent for Madame de la Luna. Her hair was spun sugar and the smell of incense lingered on the fabric of her dress. She was known for her flourishing garden and her gift at concocting herbal remedies. Some even say she has magical abilities.

She had brought her granddaughter along with her.

The first time I saw Anastacia, it felt like a dream. She stood among the rippling shadows and bursts of colours that sent pain prickling against my temples. In my fever-state, I remembered orchids wrapping around her wrist, her shoulders and her neck, carved a crude crown over her head, before its petals bloomed against her blushed cheeks. I remember the vined flowers reaching out towards me, wrapping around my arms, my legs, my chest. I remember hearing a voice, her voice perhaps, whispering my name over and over and over again. I remember her coaxing me back into waking with fingers that burned my skin, her soothing voice guiding me awake.

Lola told me I woke up calling her name.

I had been asleep for three days.

When I had finally recovered, I crossed paths with her again in the corridors of our school. Anastacia introduced herself by handing me a ripe mango. At the centre of the school courtyard was a large tree that bloomed with yellow flowers. Under its canopy, we shared the mango between us.

It was the sweetest fruit I had ever eaten.

"Nothing's changed," Anastacia murmurs beside me. We are in the plaza just outside of the church, sitting on one of the stone benches. The sun is high in the sky. She is leaning against the bark of a small tree, knees against her chest, her red and white checkered skirt pressed against her calves. We are both in our high school uniforms. Her eyes are focused on the roofs of the church peeking from the canopy. "Nothing ever does." Those golden eyes turn to me with something indecipherable. "Do you ever wonder why?"

I pluck a six-petalled santan from a shrub closest to our bench, twisting its stem between my thumb and forefinger. They say six petalled ones are rare, that they bring luck and fortune. I'm not sure I ever believed in such things. They grow along the paths in this plaza. I always find them in between a tangle of webs, but I've never seen one spider.

Anastacia turns to face me. I reach over to delicately tuck the six-petalled santan into her hair. "Not particularly."

"Aren't you curious about what's beyond?"

"Sangbulawan?" I ask. It is the name of our small barangay, named after the 'bulawan nga barko', the golden ship said to sail by the nearby river, carrying with it the souls of the dead. Bedtime stories, I thought.

She nods, leaning her chin against her knee, peering up at me with gold, gleaming eyes. I nudge the flower in her hair until it is safely tucked in between the strands.

"The ricefields."

"Further."

"The roads to the city."

"Further."

I pause. "I've never thought about it."

The smell of incense clings to my skin hours after mass and I find myself back at the de la Luna house, towards the garden hoping the strong smell of fox-gloves and jasmine will wash away the lingering smoke.

The intricate metal gate is always unlocked. It separates the garden from the rest of the house. In certain angles, the metal curls into the shape of flowers. Sometimes, I think, they look like bones.

On afternoons like this, with the sun hanging in the sky like a pendulum, the only shade is from the trees leaning over the walls, and I find myself among the fragrant flowers.

The herbal plants, the ones the Madame uses for her healing, are further back, beneath the watchful eye of a great talisay tree with a large ornate mirror nailed on its thick bark and some safely kept in a small greenhouse. I am not allowed there. Madame de la Luna says they need to be handled with a gentleness I did not yet possess.

But the flowers are everywhere and mine to care for.

Blooming clusters of asters in pastel colours. Orchids with their thin stems reaching for the sun and some wrapped around the pillars of the stone walls, curling around the fruit trees like serpents. Velvety peonies in shades of sunset, peeking from their little ceramic pots. Chrysanthemums with petals of dark magenta. Sampaguita blossoming under the shade, its deep perfume making everything feel like a dream. White and yellow frangipani, lush pink carmelias, pale orange begonias – but my favourites are the dahlias. They are spread in different corners of the garden in a variety of colours. I find myself gravitating towards a small bloom of dark red ones, their petals almost black at its centre, fading into a deep, rich red at the tips. I reach over, trailing a finger against their soft petals. They're Anastacia's favourite too.

All along the corners of the garden are different fruit trees. Starfruits with sun-yellow ripeness during summer. They pull down the branches with their weight low enough for me to pluck. Sometimes I snack on them, bite into the soft skin, sour juices sliding down my chin, in between rehoming flowers. Rambutan hang high on their branches in enticingly red clusters. Lansones mature in large, round bunches close to their branches. Sometimes Anastacia would join me in the garden with a plate of them, delicately peeling the yellow skin while watching me work. And when my fingers are too soil-stained, she would lean over and hold the translucent fruit to my lips.

The further you walk into the garden, the wilder the plants grow. I know I am close to the greenhouse when the makahiya flourish. The shy plant has leaves that droop and curl into themselves when disturbed and re-open a moment later. The older trees are here too. They have mushrooms on their branches and their barks are thick with cracks and moss. And mirrors. The Madame never speaks of them, but some trees surrounding the greenhouse have mirrors nailed to their barks.

I remember leaving a row of red roses standing along the walls, near one of the smaller fruit trees. They need replanting. They've outgrown their ceramic pots and I want them to bloom closer to their other flower siblings. I gather them in my arms, ignoring the way my reflection shimmers in the mirror and the uneasy feeling on the nape of my neck as I leave the circle of elder trees.

I take a pair of gloves lying on a wooden bench and locate a small patch of damp soil that will be perfect for their new home beside some gumamelas separated by a row of large rocks. The hole needs to be big enough for all the red roses, and bigger for them to blossom some more.

I spend the next few minutes digging with a small trowel, but soon the urge to feel the soil tingles at my fingertips. I take off the gloves and with my hands, I dig and dig and dig. I feel the dirt clinging in between my fingers. I gather some of them in between my palms. I pull at tangled dry roots until they come loose, until the soil is soft under my hands. I pluck out large stones, lay them aside for later and gently nudge the squirming worms out of the way, watch them wriggle under the pots.

I dig until my fingernails catch on something smoother, softer, whiter.

It is not the first time I have uncovered bones under this garden. I think the birds bring them in, drop them over the flower beds when they swoop low under the branches. They like to perch on the stone walls and watch over me as I work, singing along to my tuneless humming.

The white of the bone peeks from under a layer of damp soil.

"You're here again."

It's Anastacia.

I turn around in surprise, feel my finger catch on something. A pinprick of pain travels up my wrist and I hiss.

When I glance down at the hole I had dug, the bone has disappeared and in its place a lone rose sways against the afternoon breeze. My hand had grazed against one of its thorns. A thin red line runs down the side of my index finger. I press my thumbnail under the cut and watch the blood bloom.

"What's wrong?" Anastacia falls to her knees beside me, uncaring for her white dress. She takes my hand in her palm and turns it over. The blood had disappeared. "Were you tending to the roses?"

"Yes," I murmur, frowning at my hand, unblemished, unscathed. There is no pain and yet I remember the sting, remember the red line that was there just a moment ago. I nod at the row of roses sitting innocently in their pots. "They need a new home."

Anastacia hums, presses a chaste kiss against my wrist. "Come back to the House for a moment," she murmurs against my skin. Her golden eyes peer at me through long, dark lashes. "I think there's a storm coming."

And true to her word, the skies give out a low grumble.

I look up and blink against the first drop of rain on my cheek.

An uneasy silence hangs over this town. It is something that has followed me like a ghost since I was a child. Perhaps it is simply the soul a small town holds, an off-kilter, lilting thing that appears in my dreams often and without prompt.

Perhaps it's simply because this is all I've ever known — the church, the plaza, the garden and at the centre of it all, Anastacia.

A few months after I first met Anastacia, I realised that something lurked behind those golden eyes. At first, I thought it was a deep sadness.

We were the same year but had different classes and back then, I would often find myself hovering by the door of her classroom during recess, waiting for her to gather her belongings. It was then I found that not everyone found her as fascinating as I did. Instead, some of our classmates treated Anastacia with disdain.

We would find her books thrown across the playground, hidden behind trees with their pages torn and scribbled over with insults and accusations and curses. They called her a witch.

Anastacia smiled through it, but in those moments a hollowed shadow would pool under her eyes, a sadness curling on her lips. She would wrap her fingers around my wrist a little too tightly, pull me towards a clearing behind the classrooms a little too forcefully. Her skin was a little colder. But when she thought I was not looking, something akin to anger would burn in her golden eyes.

"Do you ever wish to escape?" Anastacia asks, holding a hand against her brow to peer down at me against the sunlight. She had led us into the clearing behind one of the classrooms. Our own sanctuary under the canopy of a balete tree, far enough that the sounds of the other students in the schoolyard was but a faint echo.

I hum, studying the way sunlight slipped through her fingers and pooled into her eyes. "No," I say. "It's never occurred to me."

Her strange eyes study me like a mariposa pinned onto a corkboard. "Why not?" she murmurs, before turning away, gaze returning to the trees, something nameless and dreaming in her golden eyes.

"Why would I?" I say, trying to catch her eyes. "When I have everything I need here." She turns to me then, a small furrow in between her brows. Her lips curl, as though she is on the verge of tears. There is that deep sadness again, I think, and I reach for it, tracing the shadow under her eyes, leaning closer. "What's wrong?"

She shakes her head, sniffs, and crosses the small distance between us until all I can see are the gold specks of her eyes and, when she closes them, I am drowning in the heady scent of jasmine.

Anastacia kisses like a summer storm.

At first curious – gentle fingers trailing against my warming cheeks like the heat before the first downpour of rain – then hungry, the first rumble of thunder behind gathering clouds, the first crack of lightning on earth. I lean into it, brushing my fingers against the indentations of her ribs through her shirt and I think back to the bone-keys of the de la Luna piano, how every breathless shiver feels like a song against my skin. She ends up on my lap, skirts spread against mine and fingers tangled in my hair, undoing my braids.

We only part when the ache in my lungs becomes unbearable. Her ribbons had become undone, trails behind her like blue smoke. Her lips taste sweet like ripe lansones, kiss-bitten red and slick, cheeks blooming the same shade as our favourite dahlias. We stay like that for a while, with our foreheads pressed against each other's, my hands cradling her face, the rustling of leaves and the songs of the cicadas drowning our breathless laughter.

When I pull away, my cheeks are damp with tears that are not my own.

The dahlias are the first to wilt.

I am back in the garden again. Sitting against the wall, with one hand on my lap and another against the soil. I feel spring retreating and summer's first kiss and I remember Anastacia's lips against my own. It's on my neck, the sweltering heat blooming against my nape, a warmth spreading from under the earth. The dahlias droop, as though the heat slowly sapped the vibrancy from their colours, the bounce of their leaves.

The petals are mottled with black spots, like someone has pressed their fingers against them too hard and left an archipelago of bruises in their wake. I run a finger on one of them, gently as if they might turn to ash at any moment, following the trail of bruises to their drying stems, splintering under the weight of its petals.

The dahlias have always bloomed brighter in midsummer, and flourished in the heat. I lean my head against the wall, close my eyes, wonder if they need a new home, more water, more care, more, more, more.

I only open my eyes when I hear the first lilting notes slip into the garden alongside bird song. I had left the gate open. As I walk by, I trace a finger against the rusted curves, wondering why anyone would want to carve the shape of bones on garden gates beside the flowers.

I follow the sound and find Anastacia upstairs in the antesala, sitting in front of the piano. It is a delicate thing, the de la Luna piano, all gleaming wood and shining, ivory keys. She has her back towards me, cradled in between a bookshelf and a glass case displaying a row of fine china.

"They're made of bone, you know," she says without looking back, pressing one of the white keys with a long, delicate finger.

A high note dances above our heads, sweeping past the dusty chandelier and fading into one of the many corridors. "This old thing."

"It's beautiful."

I hear her laugh. It is a breathless, hollow sound. "All dead things are, I suppose." Anastacia does not turn around. I see her shake her head, strands of hair hiding her face. Her hands move across the keys with featherlight touches.

"Will you play me a song?" I ask when the silence becomes unbearable and the only sound I can hear is my own beating heart. I sit down on the topmost stair, leaning against the bannister.

Her fingers flinch on the bone-keys before they reach for her face, swipe at the tears I do not see. When Anastacia lays her fingers against the keys once more, I close my eyes.

The house fills with a song that sounds more like a cry.

Cracks have started to appear on the mirrors that hang around the house.

I first notice them when I come to visit Anastacia, only to find the rooms empty and the garden gates wide open. There is a mirror hanging on one of the smaller talisay trees. I thought it odd, but I've seen stranger things. The mirror is round and framed with gold, curling along its circumference in a bouquet of dahlias. The reflective surface has taken the toll of time, smudged at the corners and distorted, but it is only now that I see the first crack. I trace a finger against the blooming fissure, see the same fracture crackling across my cheek.

The garden is oddly quiet. Even the stirring of leaves and the constant murmur of the living earth is muffled in my ears. I blink, catch the flicker of movement behind me and feel my heart stutter.

"Ana," I whisper, coughing against the sour fear in my throat. "You scared me." She does not say anything, only stays there, over my shoulder, studying me with those golden, indecipherable eyes. "Ana?" I make to turn around but her voice stops me.

"Please," she whispers, almost desperately. "Don't turn around."

"What is it?" The fear is tangy on my tongue now, everything in my being fighting to turn around.

"I'm sorry," she whispers and the crack in the mirror grows, splits from her jaw to her temple. "It was the only way I knew how to wake you."

I feel my heart stutter.

When I turn around, there is no-one there.

Every night, I have the same dream.

It always starts at the House.

With every step, the wood squelches beneath my shoes, damp with rot and soil. There is someone sitting by the piano, but the closer I walk, the stronger the smell of rot and wilted jasmine grows, until I feel bile rising up my throat. My knees hit the rotten floorboards. I see her approach in my periphery, blurry with tears, but I would recognise her anywhere. I raise my hand to stop her from walking any closer and she wraps her hand around mine. Her skin is cold to the touch.

"Please," Anastacia whispers wetly. I shudder, stopping myself from falling face first into the wood with my arms. When I gag, it is not bile that comes out but rotten petals – dahlias, I note vaguely – splintered stems and blood. They splatter against my wrist, stain my mouth until all I can taste is rust and the bittersweetness of flowers. Anastacia kneels before me, cold fingers tracing my jaw, tilting my head until her face splinters into view. "Please forgive me." There are tears in her eyes. "You ate the fruit," she whispers. Her hands are trembling. "The mango – I'm sorry. It was the only way to save you then but now—"

I pull away from her fingers, stumble backwards to create as much distance between us. I remember my grandmother's stories. The invisible city. Its enchanting inhabitants.

How, if a stranger in the forest offered you food, you must never eat it or you would be eternally under their enchantment.

But Anastacia was no stranger.

"You can't be—" My voice is hoarse, throat ruined by the dahlias. I cough against the blood and spit out the petals.

"I wanted to wake you. It was the only way you could remain—"

The earth lurches as another shudder wracks through my body. I fall on my back, watch the wooden beams splinter and the trees spin. Anastacia leans over me. I feel her tears fall on my cheeks like rain.

A burst of colour.

The scent of jasmine.

"No." Her voice, echoing. "No, no, no."

Every night, I have the same dream.

It always starts at the House.

The floorboards are always rotten, the walls always weep. But it is only when the makahiya leaves claw through the wood that I realise I am dreaming.

There is a story my Lola used to tell us when we were little.

It is a story about loss and about an invisible city.

I often wondered – in the curious way a child wondered – what the city would look like to me.

"Did you have a bad dream?" The swish of fabric and light streams into the room in hazy lines. I hold a hand against my eyes but someone pushes it aside. Anastacia comes into view, face stained with sunlight. She leans ever closer. Her golden eyes shine. Raindrops cling to her dark lashes and when she smiles it is soft and sad. "Is it the same one?"

BIOGRAPHIES

Edward Karshner, Professor of English at Robert Morris University, teaches courses in writing and Appalachian Literature. His research explores the roots of Appalachian folklore, magic, and mysticism. A 2022 Research Fellow in Folklore at Berea College's Special Collections and Archives, Karshner is the author of "These Stories Sustain Me" in the collection *Appalachian Reckoning: A Region Replies to Hillbilly Elegy*. His creative non-fiction appears in the on-line magazine Reckon Review where he is a recurring columnist and the Appalachian culture blog Blind Pig and the Acorn. His short fiction has appeared in numerous anthologies and in *Still: The Journal*.

Lerah Mae Barcenilla grew up in Cuartero, Capiz in the Philippines full of magic, superstition and tradition before moving to the UK. Her work touches on topics of the diaspora, memory, mythology, folklore and the state of duality. Her writing has appeared in Harana Poetry, with Verve Poetry Press, was Highly Commended in The Literary Consultancy's PEN Factor Award—Novel (2021) and won the Creative Future Writers Award—Platinum Poetry (2022). When she is not writing, she works as a marketing officer for the charity responsible for two of Birmingham's iconic concert halls and as a researcher for Maniwala Movement, an Instagram account sharing resources on the cultures, customs and beliefs of pre-colonial Philippines.

Fiction by Michael Bird has been published constantly over the last few years, most recently on urban witchcraft, 'The New Client', in Panel Magazine, (Budapest, 2023), on deranged fandom, 'I Named Every Donut in My Shop After Scorsese Movies. No One Bought The Departed', in Daily Drunk

Mag (New Orleans, 2023), and on family politics during the pandemic, 'A Drive Through the Park', in Porter House Review (Austin, Texas, 2022). Mixed media 'These Walls of Me' was Winner of Second Prize on www.theshortstory.net (UK, 2018), and he has also been published by British journals and sites Lune, Grist, Storgy, Bandit Fiction, and in two anthologies of the annual Bristol Short Story Prize. In 2022, his body horror story about a McDonald's mascot from the 80s, 'Fry Girl 4 Eva' (USA), was nominated for a Pushcart Prize. He also works as an investigative and narrative journalist, with features published on organised crime, stray dogs, vampire-hunters, killer home-made drugs, food emergencies, the war in Ukraine and organic farming.

Rose Biggin is a writer and theatre performer living in London. Her short fiction has appeared in various anthologies, made the recommended reading list for Best of British Fantasy, and won the Dark Sire Gothic Fiction Prize; her first story collection is forthcoming from NewCon Press. Her novels are punk fantasy Wild Time (Surface Press) and gothic thriller The Belladonna Invitation (Ghost Orchid Press), and she is an associate lecturer in Creative Writing at Birkbeck.

Pete Hartley boasts an extensive writing career with numerous accolades, including winning the BBC Radio North West Playwriting Competition and the Cheshire Community Council playwriting competition. His plays, such as "Making the Grade" and "Gertie and the Guild Machine", have received critical acclaim and have been produced in various venues. Biographica

Lauren Archer is a writer of the gothic, surreal and strange based in Liverpool, UK. Her short story 'Out of Water' was published by Crow and Cross Keys literary journal. In 2022, her short story 'The Allotment' was longlisted for the Mslexia Short Story Prize.

About Fly on the Wall Press

A publisher with a conscience.
Political, Sustainable, Ethical.
Publishing politically-engaged, international fiction, poetry and cross-genre anthologies on pressing issues. Founded in 2018 by founding editor, Isabelle Kenyon.

Some other publications:

The Sound of the Earth Singing to Herself by Ricky Ray

We Saw It All Happen by Julian Bishop

The Unpicking by Donna Moore

Imperfect Beginnings by Viv Fogel

These Mothers of Gods by Rachel Bower

Sin Is Due To Open In A Room Above Kitty's by Morag Anderson

Fauna by David Hartley

How To Bring Him Back by Clare HM

The Process of Poetry Edited by Rosanna McGlone

Snapshots of the Apocalypse by Katy Wimhurst

Demos Rising Edited by Isabelle Kenyon

Exposition Ladies by Helen Bowie

A Dedication to Drowning by Maeve McKenna

The House with Two Letterboxes by Janet H Swinney

Climacteric by Jo Bratten

The State of Us by Charlie Hill

The Sleepless by Liam Bell

Social Media:

@fly_press (Twitter) @flyonthewallpress (Instagram and Tiktok)

@flyonthewallpress (Facebook)

www.flyonthewallpress.co.uk